Countdown to Valentine's Day

Dianna Houx

Contents

-Days till Valentine's Day-

Nineteen

"Nineteen days till Valentine's Day," Grace groaned as she handed Molly a glass of lemonade. After pouring a second glass for herself, she sat at the table across from her new friend. "I can't believe an entire month has passed since the guests from our Old-Fashioned Christmas Experience left. I feel like I'm still in recovery from all the stress."

"Seems pretty understandable considering all that has happened in the last four weeks." She held up her index finger to illustrate. "First, you had to put away all the Christmas decorations, which was as big of an undertaking as putting them up. Second, you had to clean the house from top to bottom. Third, you had to find homes for all the puppies, deal with replacing the broken furnace, prepare for a permanent house guest, and take care of Gladys after she had that fall. That's a lot for one person to handle."

"I suppose you're right. I'm just glad you're back. I'm really sorry the deal on the house you and Grant were buying fell through, but I'm relieved you've moved in with Gladys for the time being. Knowing she's not alone, especially at night, has taken a load off my back," Grace said with a shake of her head. "Breaking a hip sure does suck."

Molly crinkled her nose. "Yeah, it does," she replied as she stared into space. After a moment, she shook her head as if to clear it. "Anyway, the big question is, what will we do for Valentine's Day?"

"I wish we could skip this holiday and focus on getting everyone well. Granny is doing better but is still in recovery. Now that Gladys has broken her hip, it feels too much to add a group of guests, let alone activities. Not to mention, we're already a day behind when we started last time."

Molly smiled sympathetically and reached across the table to pat Grace's hand. "I understand, but you took quite the financial hit with the furnace replacement. Not to mention the taxes you're going to have to pay. Even with Hunter's rent, money will get tight really quick if we don't jump on this opportunity, and don't forget, the next holiday won't be rolling around for another two and a half months."

Grace groaned again. "Okay, fine; from now on, you can call me Miss Responsibility."

Molly laughed. "How about you show yourself some actual grace instead, and this time, ask for and accept the help you need? I'll be with you every step of the way."

"That definitely helps," Grace sighed. "Valentine's Day is on a Tuesday this year. How do we handle that? Do you think anyone will even want to book a vacation this close to the beginning of the year?"

"We'll have less time for planned events, and people will only want to stay for five days instead of ten, but I think it's still doable."

"If we cut the booked time in half, the price will also have to be cut in half. It's less work but a lot less money, too," Grace said, concerned.

"Not necessarily. People pay for the experience. Experience does not have to equal the number of days they spend here."

"Maybe," Grace drawled out. "I don't know. I feel like if we're going to go for the experience factor, then we need to do something different." She thought about it for a couple of minutes. "Everybody always focuses on couples this time of year. What if we do the opposite and focus on single people instead?"

"Like, as in a getaway from all the romance? Or, as in, we play matchmaker?"

Grace gave it some more thought. "I'm thinking neither. We still offer fun Valentine's Day-themed activities, but we offer packages for singles to treat themselves instead. Think spa days, singles mixers, chocolate fountains, that sort of thing."

"Ooh, we could do one of those murder mystery dinners. You could even sell tickets to some locals as well. That would be a fun way to make some extra money."

"Isn't that more of a Halloween kind of thing?" Grace asked a bit skeptically.

Molly shrugged. "I'm pretty sure they do them year-round. Grant and I went to one years ago around this time. Even if they don't, it will be one more way in which we'll stand out."

"Sounds like we're getting somewhere. The other town council members might have some ideas as well."

"Actually, we have a meeting with Mayor Allen this afternoon. We don't have time to wait until the next council meeting."

Grace gave another defeated sigh. "Okay. Looks like it's full steam ahead, then."

Molly narrowed her eyes as she studied her friend. "Grace, what's going on? You're normally a very upbeat and positive person. Is something wrong with Granny?"

She shook her head. "Granny's okay. I'm just tired, that's all."

"Is it Hunter? Have you guys had a fight?"

"We haven't had the chance to have a fight. He was supposed to be back two weeks ago, but as of today, he's still in New York. Honestly, I think he's changed his mind about moving down here," Grace replied, her voice wavering as tears threatened to flood her eyes.

"Oh honey, I'm sure that's not true. It just takes time to wrap up all the loose ends. Especially when the decision to move is as sudden as this one was. Remember, Grant and I just got back a couple of days ago."

"That may be true, but we haven't talked on the phone in weeks. He's only texted me twice to let me know he wouldn't be showing up as planned. Every time I text him, he leaves me on read." Grace shook her head sadly. "I'm sure once he got back to New York, the allure of our small town wore off pretty fast."

"Why don't I talk to Grant and see what he knows? If Hunter has had a change of heart, as his business partner, Grant would be the first to know."

"Thanks, Molly." Grace tried to smile while holding back tears. She wanted to believe that Molly was right, but it was tough. Most people want to move out of small towns; the glitz and glamour of big-city life, especially in cities like New York City, is hard to resist. Very few want to go in the opposite direction.

Small towns are fun to visit. Their charm and 'old-fashioned' ways are a fun escape from the busyness of everyday life. But the lack of conveniences, long drives every time you need to go somewhere, and low employment opportunities usually dissuaded people from doing more than just visiting. She probably shouldn't have mentioned that when talking to Hunter before he left. Grace couldn't imagine living anywhere else. Having lived in Winterwood her whole life, she considered it her home, but it was another story for Hunter.

With another small sigh, she got up and put the lemonade glasses in the sink. It wasn't just the fact losing Hunter hurt her personally. It was the fact they would lose his rent money, too. One more room would likely be available for the next 'Experience,' but that money would not compensate for months' worth of lost rent.

Oh well, she couldn't worry about that right now. Whether she liked it or not, it was time to open the bed and breakfast again. She owed it to her potential guests to put all her time and energy into making it the best experience they ever had. The stuff with Hunter could wait.

***

Grace and Molly filed into Mayor Allen's office later that afternoon. They had spent the rest of the morning fine-tuning their latest plan and were excited to discuss it with him; they were more than a little surprised when they got there and discovered the other council members were there, too.

"Ladies, thank you both for coming," Mayor Allen said as he beamed at them.

"We hope you don't mind us all butting in," said Bea. "When we heard you two wanted to discuss a new idea with the Mayor, we got a little excited," she said with a laugh.

Molly smiled at them. "Actually, we're glad you're all here. You've saved us the hassle of tracking you down individually."

"Wonderful," the mayor said as he clapped his hands. "Let's get this meeting started, shall we?"

Molly looked at Grace. "Would you like me to do the presentation?"

Grace nodded, grateful for the opportunity to blend into the background again. While her previous experience had given her a much-needed push out of her comfort zone, she still did not relish being the center of attention, even in a small group like this.

"As you all know, the Christmas Experience the town put together was a huge success." Molly looked around the room, and when she saw everyone nodded in agreement, she continued. "Grace and I would like to do another experience, this time for Valentine's Day."

"Will this be for couples?" asked Bea.

Molly shook her head. "This time, we will focus our attention on single people. Since they are a highly overlooked group this time of year, we think we will have a lot of success if we cater to them specifically."

"I'm not sure I understand," said Addie. "Why do single people care about Valentine's Day?"

"They probably don't, but they're also probably sick and tired of being reminded that they're single and made to feel bad about it on top of it. We want to do the opposite. We want to celebrate the fact they're single."

"How will we do that?" asked Junior. "More importantly, can we make any money doing it?"

Molly took a deep breath. "We will offer unique packages to guests who book a stay at Grace's bed-and-breakfast. We plan to offer 'spa packages' using some vendors around town. We will, of course, need the food services of Addie and Bea," she said as she looked at them directly. Thankfully, both of them nodded in agreement.

"As for the town, we plan to host a murder mystery dinner on the Saturday before Valentine's Day. We will sell tickets and open them up to locals and the people in the surrounding towns. This plan will require all the downtown business owners to agree to be involved."

"What do you need from us?" asked Mr. Wilkins.

"For an event this big, we're going to need a lot of locations to send the people for clues. Also, we will need volunteers to act out the actual mystery. Since we don't have a large enough building to host a dinner for that many people, we'll need to set up serving stations around town.

"This sounds like a lot of work," grumbled Junior.

Molly nodded her head. "It is definitely going to require a lot of work, but Grace and I will do the bulk of it. We've broken down everything we need into small categories," she replied, handing everyone a list. "All we need you to do is your one small part."

It was silent for a few minutes as everyone read over their copy of Molly's list. Graced watched from her seat in the corner, attempting to read the expressions on their faces. She really hoped everyone would agree to the plan. At first, it had seemed overwhelming to her, but the more she and Molly had discussed it, the more excited she had become.

Finally, Bea looked up and smiled. "This looks awesome! I bet we'll sell hundreds of tickets with the right marketing!"

"That's the plan," Molly said, smiling back. "Not only that, we'll get tons of people into your stores that haven't been there before. This will be a great opportunity to showcase what you have to offer." She pointedly looked at Mr. Wilkins, who looked thrilled to hear that.

"Do we need to decorate again?" asked Addie. "I already had a lot of Christmas stuff. I don't have much in the way of Valentine's Day decorations."

"Do as much as you can," said Molly. "It will be nice to look festive, but this holiday isn't as decoration-dependent as Christmas. Besides, we're trying not to throw the lovey-dovey aspect of the holiday into these people's faces."

"This all sounds very exciting, ladies," said Mayor Allen. "There's just one question. What will you do on the actual day of the holiday?"

Molly gave Grace a nervous look. This was the one part they weren't sure about. "We were thinking we would hold a single's mixer. We would invite all the singles from the local area to a social event. We would serve drinks, play music, have a buffet, that sort of thing. At the end of the night, we would have an auction. All the proceeds would go to the park fund you've been trying to raise money for."

"What kind of auction?" asked Junior suspiciously.

"We'll ask businesses for donations, of course, but if we can get some volunteers, we thought it might be fun to auction off some men for dates or handyman projects. That part is up in the air," Molly said with a shrug of her shoulders.

"We're going to have to give that some serious thought," said Mayor Allen. "We don't want to do anything that could endanger someone or cause hurt feelings."

"It will definitely require a delicate touch," Molly agreed. "But if done right, it could be a lot of fun and raise a lot of money. We have time to work out the details before making a final decision."

"Do you think we need to round up the town and get everyone involved again?" asked Bea.

"Not as of yet," Molly replied. "Our main focus is on local business owners this time."

Mayor Allen clapped his hands. "It looks like we have a fairly solid plan. Why don't we dismiss for the day and meet again tomorrow? That should give everyone enough time to come up with any questions or concerns they need addressed."

After some excited goodbyes and exclamations, the crowd dispersed. Molly and Grace got back in the car, each breathing a sigh of relief.

"I think that went well," Molly told Grace as she started the car.

"Better than I expected. Guess it's back to planning our marketing campaign."

"That's the fun part," Molly replied with a laugh. "Eventually, you're going to learn to love it too."

"If you say so..." Grace trailed off, then laughed to not hurt Molly's feelings. She would never love marketing but would always be thankful for her new friend.

-Days till Valentine's Day-

Eighteen

"Do you think it's strange I don't feel as much stress and pressure this time?" Grace asked Molly. "Have I already become apathetic?" She walked around Molly's new office in the building Grant had rented. It was located about five blocks down the street from where they lived.

"I'm pretty sure the fact you're asking means you have not become apathetic," she replied as she rolled her eyes. "Seriously, you need to relax."

Grace shrugged as she continued her inspection. The building had been vacant for as long as she could remember. At one point, it had been a warehouse that employed hundreds of people. Somewhere over the decades, it had been remodeled and turned into a large office complex. To her knowledge, Grant was the first person to rent it since the remodel. "This place is really nice. Kind of big, though. Do you guys plan to hire a lot of people?"

"We need at least three offices and a conference room. We'll probably need space for an administrative assistant at some point," Molly replied thoughtfully. "If the business takes off, we'll likely need even more staff. So yeah, I could see us filling this place up."

"Wow! That would be great for the town. I bet Mayor Allen was practically drooling over the potential tax revenue."

Molly laughed. "I'm sure he was. In all fairness, though, this really is a win-win for everyone. Do you know how much a building this size would cost in a city like Boston? We'd end up bankrupt before we could book our first client."

Grace thought about what she said, then turned to face her. "You said three offices. Does that mean Hunter's still planning to come?"

Molly winced and then sighed. "As far as Grant knows, yes. But he admitted he hadn't heard from Hunter in at least a week. I'm sorry, Grace, it seems Hunter has ghosted all of us. I'm sure it's just for now," she added quickly.

Grace tried to smile at Molly's thoughtfulness. "It's okay. I'm starting to come to terms with the fact I might never see him again. It's my fault, anyway. I just hope his change of plans won't negatively impact your new business."

"In what way is it your fault?" Molly asked, her eyes narrowed as she scrutinized Grace from behind her desk.

Grace took a deep breath and let it out slowly. "Before he left, Hunter and I talked about what it would be like when he moved down here permanently. He really loved that truck he rented and said he planned to buy one. I pointed out that trucks get pretty low gas mileage and said he might want to consider getting something more practical since he'll need to drive up to the city a lot. He got pretty quiet after that."

"I don't see how you pointing out something practical makes his change of heart your fault."

"The reason Hunter came here in the first place was to immerse himself in our small-town country way of life. The truck was a huge part of that. I'm pretty sure when I brought up how impractical driving said truck every day would be, I shattered the image he had created in his mind of his new life," Grace shrugged. "I don't know. It sounds silly and shallow, but there is a big difference between living in the country and vacationing there. I think I opened his eyes to that."

Molly stared at her for a couple of minutes with a thoughtful expression. "I know this will sound harsh, so I want you to know I'm saying this as your friend. If Hunter's desire to live here was so tenuous that a truck caused him to change his mind, you are better off discovering that now. There are a lot of good men out there, Grace. It hurts now, but Hunter was not your only chance at love."

"I'm not sure you've noticed, but we're fresh out of eligible bachelors around here. From where I'm sitting, he literally was my only chance at love," said Grace. She tried to sound like she was joking but couldn't quite pull it off. The sad truth is it wasn't a joke. Long-distance relationships were difficult to pull off. It took forty-five minutes to drive to the nearest big city. That might not seem like a lot, but you might as well be forty-five hours away. People are busy. No one wants to travel all the time just to hang out.

"Let's just see how things go. We're about to host an event for single people. Maybe Mr. Right will be one of the ones that show up!" Molly replied cheerfully.

Grace rolled her eyes. "Speaking of events, we should talk to the business owners about the spa package. Unless you want me to go by myself?"

"No, I'll come with you. I haven't met these ladies before and look forward to getting to know them."

"Hey, Molly?" Grant called out from the office next door.

"Yeah," she shouted back.

A minute later, he appeared in the doorway. "Oh good, you're both here," he said, addressing them. "I just got a call from Hunter. His plane arrives Sunday afternoon, so he plans to get here sometime that night."

Grace looked at him with her mouth open in shock. "Does he plan to stay at my house?"

"It sounded like it. He said to tell you he's sorry, he's been swamped, but he'll talk to you when he gets here."

Grace looked at Molly to see her reaction to the news, but her face was an unreadable mask. "I'm not sure how to feel about this. He has enough time to call Grant and talk to him but not enough to send me a simple text message? I may not be an expert on relationships, but even I can see this isn't how things should work."

Molly stood up and walked around her desk, linking her arm through Grace's when she reached her. "Let's not worry about it right now. Give him a chance to explain when he gets here. If you're unsatisfied with his answer, then you can figure out what to do."

Grace nodded. "That sounds practical. Ready to go?"

"Yep." She kissed Grant on the cheek as they walked past him out the door. "Later, babe," she called out behind her.

"Later," he waved.

***

When they arrived at their first stop, Molly sat in the car, staring at the sign. "Lulu's Hair and Nail Salon. It's definitely short and to the point," she pointed out.

"They've been in business for at least twenty years. I remember coming here when I was a little girl. It used to be owned by Lulu, but she retired a few years ago. Her daughter Lula runs it now."

"Lulu and Lula?" Molly asked, her eyebrows raised.

Grace shrugged. "Family name, I think. Anyway, Lula's nice in a quirky sort of way. Never heard a bad word about her."

"Sounds great. Maybe she'll have some ideas on how to spice up our package."

They got out of the car, walked inside, and were immediately greeted by Lula, who was cutting the hair of Chrissy, the local boutique owner.

"Grace! It's good to see you," Lula exclaimed.

"Hi, Grace," Chrissy waved from her chair.

"Hi, ladies, it's good to see you both," replied Grace. "This is my friend Molly. She just moved here with her husband, Grant."

"Oh yeah, you're Mandy's niece," said Lula. "It's nice to meet you. Do you need a haircut?"

Molly smiled at the woman. "It's nice to meet you, too. I don't need a haircut today, but when I do, I'll be sure to book an appointment."

"What can we do for you, then?" Lula asked.

Molly looked at Grace again, who nodded at her to go ahead with their questions. "Grace and I plan to open the bed-and-breakfast again for a Valentine's Day Experience. We would love to offer a spa package for our guests and would like to know if you would be interested in participating?"

"Is this, like, for couples or something?" asked Lula

"No, it's going to be for singles," Molly replied. "We thought they could come here for their nails and then go to Amy's for a massage. What do you think?"

"What day are you thinking?"

"Probably Saturday. If that's a busy day for you, we can change it. We just thought it might be a nice thing for the guests to do before the big murder mystery dinner that night."

Lula's face lit up. "Y'all are putting on a murder mystery? I love those. Can we all come, or is it for guests only?"

"We'll be selling tickets to the public, so of course, you're both welcome to purchase one and come," Molly replied.

"Awesome!" she pumped her fist in the air. "You know what we could do," she drawled. "The guests could start by getting a massage. Then, they could come here and get their hair and nails done. Afterward, they could head to Chrissy's and pick a new outfit. It will make the whole thing feel more special."

Molly and Grace looked at each other as big grins spread over their faces.

"Now that's something I could sell," Molly told her excitedly.

"What if I offer a glass of wine while they shop like some of those high-end clothing stores do?" Chrissy asked as she jumped on the idea bandwagon.

"Ooh, I could offer wine, too," said Lula. "And maybe some chocolate while they're getting their nails done. If that doesn't say 'treat yourself,' I don't know what does!"

"These are fantastic ideas, ladies," said Molly. "Are you sure they won't interfere with your regular customers?"

"Saturdays are appointment only for me," Lula replied. "So, I'll be able to control who's in here. And who knows, maybe I'll run some kind of Valentine's Day special, and everyone will get special treatment that day."

"I think I'll do something like that, too," said Chrissy. "If the murder mystery is open to the public, maybe I can drum up some business from some locals,"

"I would be willing to help both of you advertise if you'd like?" Molly offered.

"You'll need to be prepared for an onslaught of customers," said Grace. "Y'all know how it is around here; people go all out for these big events,"

"You're right," Chrissy replied. "I might need to hire some extra help for the day, but it would be so worth it if I could draw a big crowd."

"This has been great," Molly said with a smile. "I'm going to add both of you to the marketing campaign I'm putting together. Grace and I will contact you in the next few days to review the final copy." Molly shook both of their hands and turned to leave.

Grace waved goodbye and followed her out the door. Once they were back in the car, she turned to Molly. "That went better than I expected," she said.

Molly nodded excitedly. "They had some great ideas. I think people will love this new experience we're putting together. We'll probably sell out in hours."

"I kind of wish we had more than just four rooms available," Grace laughed. "This actually sounds pretty fun!"

"Don't worry about the number of rooms. We're going to have plenty of people and make plenty of money," Molly reassured her.

"On to Amy's?" Molly asked.

"Yep, I can't wait to see what she has to offer."

They went to Amy's, but unfortunately, she had already gone home for the day. Her phone number was listed on the door, but it went straight to voicemail when they called. Grace considered leaving a message but ultimately decided to just come back later.

With their two main tasks for the day done, Molly returned to work, and Grace went home to check on Granny and Gladys. Things were coming together better than she had hoped; she just wished her personal life would work out as well as her professional one. Although, before all of this started, she had neither. It may be time to focus on the positive instead of the negative.

-Days till Valentine's Day-

Seventeen

Grace awoke to the sound of voices in the foyer downstairs. A quick peek at the clock on the table beside her bed showed it was already nine o'clock in the morning. Groaning, she sat up and tried to rub the sleep from her eyes. It had taken hours for her to fall asleep the night before, and if she was honest, she could still use a couple more to feel rested.

When she could delay the inevitable no longer, she dragged herself out of bed and walked over to the window. It was dark and dreary outside, the sun completely hidden from view. A cold wind blew in through the drafty old windows. The weather was definitely befitting her mood.

After pulling on jeans and a sweatshirt, she greeted Molly, Grant, and Gladys downstairs. It had become part of their morning routine to drop Gladys off before heading to work. Gladys liked to spend the day with Granny, and having them both in the same place made things much easier on Grace.

By the time she made it downstairs, they had already helped Gladys into bed next to Granny.

"Good morning, everyone," Grace called out with a cheerfulness she did not feel. She grabbed a couple of extra blankets and got to work, wrapping them around the shoulders of each of the elderly women. "It's very chilly outside. Looks like we might get more snow soon."

Molly clapped her hands together. "I just love the snow. It makes everything feel so magical," she said dreamily.

Grace gave her a sideways look. "You sure are in a good mood this morning."

"Molly," Grant said in a warning tone of voice.

"Oh hush, these people are family. You can't expect me to keep this a secret from family, can you?"

Grant sighed, then gave his wife a big smile. "I guess you're right. Go ahead and tell them."

"Tell us what? I'm confused," Grace interrupted. Whatever was going on was clearly good news for them, but that didn't mean it would be good for everyone else. Did they find a new house? Were they planning to move far away? The fear of being abandoned once more slammed into her so hard it took her breath away.

"Grace," Molly called her name. She grabbed Grace by the arm and led her to a chair, practically pushing her down into it. "Are you okay? You look like you're about to faint."

Grace looked up into Molly's concerned face. It took a minute for her to register what was happening, but once she did, she could feel her cheeks heat with embarrassment. A glance around the room showed all eyes on her, and she immediately felt ashamed for interrupting Molly's big announcement. "I'm so sorry. I don't know what came over me. Please continue."

"My big news can wait. Right now, I'm worried about you."

She shook her head. "I'm fine, really. I just got a little dizzy. I may have stood up too fast or something." Grace smiled up at her to prove she was okay. "Please tell us your news." Being forced to wait for bad news was much worse than being told outright. It's like ripping off a bandaid. The fear of pain is always worse than the actual pain.

Molly looked unsure about continuing her announcement, causing Grace to feel even worse. She had ruined her friend's big moment. It may not have been on purpose, but that didn't change the fact she had done it. Some friend she was turning out to be.

"Well," Molly began, somewhat nervously. "Grant and I are having a baby!"

The room was so silent you could hear a pin drop. When the realization that she was not losing her new friends finally sank in, Grace jumped up and threw her arms around Molly, squealing with joy as she did so. "I'm so happy for you both!"

"That's wonderful news," said Granny, a tear glistening in her eye.

They all turned to stare at Gladys, who had gone unusually quiet. When she still didn't speak, Molly let go of Grace and went to sit next to her on the bed, taking the woman's hands in hers. "Is everything okay? If you're worried about a new baby bothering you, I'm sure we'll be able to find a new place to live long before the baby comes."

"It's not that, dear. Quite the opposite, actually."

Molly tilted her head to the side. "I'm not sure I understand."

"I know this is sudden, but I am very fond of you and Grant. I'm tickled pink at the two of you becoming parents. The thing is, I don't want you to move. I want you and the new little one to stay with me." Gladys wiped the tears from her eyes, gratefully accepting a tissue from Granny.

"We love you too, Gladys, and would love to stay with you. But we're going to need our own place," Grant said gently.

"The house is huge. It's too big for a single old woman to manage on her own but plenty big for a family. You'll have the entire second floor to yourselves, and I'm sure we can find a way to share the downstairs living spaces."

Grace was wholly on board with this plan and jumped in to help convince them. "Don't forget how close Gladys's house is to your new office. Plus, Molly will have plenty of people to keep her company when you need to go out of town," Grace said to Grant.

It was the last part that caught Grant's attention. "I hadn't thought about leaving Molly alone when I travel for business. She's a capable woman, but in her condition, it would be helpful to know there's someone nearby if something were to happen."

"Are you sure this is what you want, Gladys? We don't want you to feel like we're taking advantage of your generosity," asked Molly.

"I've never been more sure. We old people need a reason to get out of bed in the morning. You three have really changed things around here for the better. I don't want to lose that."

"I don't either," Granny chimed in. "I think we've all been good for each other, and this new arrangement seems to work out for everyone."

Molly looked at Grant, who nodded his head. When she turned back to look at Gladys, there were tears in her eyes. "You guys are all so sweet. I don't think I have ever felt more welcomed and cared for in my entire life. Thank you all so much." She grabbed Gladys's hands again. "And thank you for welcoming us into your home. We would love to stay with you."

Gladys patted her cheek lovingly. "I'm delighted to hear that. Now, let's talk about your newest plan. We've heard you guys are putting on a murder mystery."

Molly laughed. "Two weeks from tonight. We're pretty certain it's going to be a huge hit!"

"We're sure it is, too, which is why we want to be a part of it."

"Oh? What would you like to do?"

"Well, you're going to need a killer and a victim, right?" she paused while Molly nodded in agreement. "I want to be the victim, and Granny wants to be the killer. It'll be a hoot!"

Grace struggled to keep from laughing, the image of Granny killing Gladys too absurd. "No one is going to believe that Granny killed you, Gladys," Grace said, hiding her smile behind her hand.

"That's what makes it the perfect crime. No one will suspect my dearest friend was willing to off me in a fit of rage."

"What's her motive?" Grace asked, no longer capable of hiding her laughter.

"She snores," Granny said matter-of-factly.

All three laughed, the look on Granny's face too funny to ignore. "Well, she does," Granny replied defensively. "An old lady like me needs her beauty rest, and that's not happening with the walrus over here. Her snoring could wake the dead."

"Which is the only reason you're still alive," Gladys cracked back. "You should be thanking me!"

Grace laughed some more, shaking her head at their banter. "We do need a couple of volunteers..." she told Molly.

Molly shrugged. "Works for me. We'll just have to ensure we have security around that night if we're going to have a bunch of strangers showing up."

"I can help arrange that," said Grant, amusement dancing in his eyes.

"Good, I'm glad that's settled. Now, if you kids will excuse us, we've got a movie coming on we've been dying to see." Gladys picked up the remote control and started surfing through the channels.

Realizing they'd been dismissed, they filed out of the room.

"Those two sure are funny," said Grant as he kissed his wife. "I'm going to head over to the office. I'll see you at lunch."

Molly hugged him before saying goodbye, a look of adoration clear on her face. "Those two remind me of someone. I just can't quite put my finger on who," she mused.

"Dorothy and Rose?" Grace asked innocently. "You know, from the Golden Girls," she said when Molly gave her a strange look. "Or were you thinking more like Thelma and Louise?"

Molly laughed. "Both! Thelma and Louise when they were younger, and Dorothy and Rose now. Although Dorothy and Sophia might be more accurate."

"Better not let them hear you say that. They'll spend weeks arguing over which one is Sophia. And don't for a second think they won't play that up, too!"

"We can still hear you," Granny called out from the other room.

Grace shook her head in mock indignation. "Look what you've done!"

They could hear laughter coming from the bedroom, which made them laugh, too.

"In all seriousness, I'm really happy for you and Grant. I know how badly you wanted to have a baby."

Molly gave her a big hug. "Thank you. It's still early, though; I just found out last night. We decided to wait until we got through the first trimester to tell anyone, but as soon as I saw you guys this morning, I just couldn't hold it in."

"I'm pretty sure I would find news this exciting hard to keep to myself, too," Grace smiled reassuringly.

"Are you sure you're okay? You went white as a sheet when I said I had an announcement to make."

Grace wanted to lie, was planning to lie, but ultimately told the truth. She
would never get through her issues if she pretended
they didn't exist. "I thought you were going to announce you're moving away. I'm afraid my fear of abandonment reared its ugly head."

"Oh, Grace. I'm sorry. But why would you automatically assume we're leaving? We just moved here and rented that large office down the street."

"The sale of your house fell through," Grace said as she sighed. Running her hands through her hair, she tried to think of a reason that made sense for her earlier jump to the wrong conclusion. "Things were hard before you showed up last month. Then they got better. Then they got hard again when you returned to Boston to pack your things. When you came back, things were good again. I think the fear of you leaving and things returning to being hard is raw and prominent right now."

"I can see how that makes sense."

"Despite that, I'm really sorry. My behavior was selfish, and I ruined a big moment for you. I do hope you'll forgive me." Grace bowed her head in shame, unable to look her friend in the eye.

Lifting her chin with her finger, Molly forced her to look at her. "You didn't do anything wrong. You're allowed to have feelings, Grace. If you need forgiveness, you have it, but know I honestly don't believe there's anything to forgive."

Grace hugged her friend, relief washing over her. "Thank you."

Molly patted her on the back. "You're welcome. If you ever need to talk, please come to me, okay?" she stepped back so she could see Grace as she nodded. "Good. How about we have a cup of tea with those leftover scones I saw on the counter when we came in? I've been craving one of those all morning!"

"You're having pregnancy cravings already?"

"No. Bea's scones are just that good!"

They laughed as they headed to the kitchen. It was kind of crazy how quickly a bad day could turn into a good one when you allowed your loved ones in. A lesson she was very thankful she was starting to learn.

-Days till Valentine's Day-

Sixteen

"One hot coffee, one tea, and two breakfast platters," Grace said as she laid the items on Molly's desk. "I can't believe you guys are working on Sunday," Grace tsked.

"Why are you delivering breakfast?" asked Molly.

"I've been working on my cooking skills, and I need guinea pigs to be my taste testers," Grace replied. "Breakfast seemed the easiest place to start. Although I did manage to burn cereal once, so even breakfast might be too ambitious for the culinary challenged."

"You burned cereal?" Molly's eyes went wide with shock. "How on earth did you manage that?"

"I was boiling water for Granny's tea and set the bowl of cereal too close to the burner. It was an absentminded accident, but one that keeps getting brought up every time I try to cook." Grace rolled her eyes. "Anyway, I made french toast, bacon, and scrambled eggs. Try it and let me know what you think."

Molly looked unsure but was kind enough to reach for a container. After cutting a bite-sized piece of french toast, she raised it to her nose and sniffed it. "It smells good," she said before putting it in her mouth.

Grace watched closely, holding her breath while she waited for the verdict. She had watched a lot of YouTube videos on how to make the best french toast and had spent hours practicing before she finally felt she had something good enough to serve others. It would be really disappointing if her skills were still found lacking after all her hard work.

"Mmm, this is actually really good," Molly finally said. "Like, really, really good."

"You don't have to sound so surprised," Grace pouted.

"Hey, don't blame me. You're the one who set the bar by telling me your burned cereal story. Seriously, though, I would pay to have this again. What's your secret?"

Grace shrugged. "I combined a couple of the recipes I found online. Do you really think it will be good enough to serve guests? Bea is concerned she won't have enough time for breakfast each day, with the holiday and all."

"I think the guests will go crazy over it," she said as she took a bite of the scrambled eggs. "These eggs are good, too," she said thoughtfully. After chewing for a couple of minutes, she continued. "It's the seasoning. Whatever you used to season the food this morning, it's completely transformed the dishes. You might have just discovered your inner Julia Child."

"Wow, really? It's that good?" Grace asked in surprise. "All I could bring myself to hope for was that it wouldn't kill you."

"You really need to learn to give yourself more credit. You're a lot more talented than you think. And yes, it really is that good."

"Thanks, Molly. That means a lot to me."

"Ladies, guess what?" Grant asked excitedly as he rushed through the door. "That old railroad hotel is going up for sale in a couple of weeks," he said before they could guess.

"Really?" asked Grace. "How do you know?"

"I just came back from a little impromptu meeting with Mayor Allen. The owners have listed the hotel with his real estate agency, so he's got firsthand knowledge of all the details."

"Okay, but why are you so excited about it?" asked Molly.

"This could be a golden opportunity for us," he replied, moving his hand in a circular motion to indicate the three of them.

"I'm not sure I understand," started Grace, confusion evident on her face. "How is an old hotel, in an extreme state of disrepair, a golden opportunity?"

"Think about it. You guys are selling these high-end experience packages, but only four bedrooms are available at Grace's. Imagine what you could do if there were twenty more rooms available."

"You want us to buy the hotel and open it back up for business?" Grace asked incredulously. "It's been at least sixty years since they closed down. From what I've heard, the place isn't even habitable anymore."

"I know all that but think about it. If we don't act on this, someone else will. Someone who sees the efforts you're making to revitalize the town, and they will be the ones to reap all the benefits of your hard work."

Grace pinched the space between her eyes. She could feel a headache coming on. "I never intended to revitalize the town, nor does it need revitalizing. We've only had one successful run with our bed-and-breakfast campaign. That hardly justifies the enormous expense of buying and renovating a large three-story decrepit hotel."

"Your success is the reason the owners have decided to sell. When they tried to sell in the past, they couldn't find a buyer. They're convinced this time will be different." Grant walked over to Molly and pulled her into his arms. "Imagine the possibilities," he said as he danced her around the room.

Molly laughed as she twirled in his arms. "What has gotten into you?" she asked as he dipped her low and then pulled her back up close to him.

"I don't know," he said as he shrugged. "Something inside just clicked when I heard the news. I really think this could be a great opportunity. It might even be why the sale of the house we planned to buy fell through. There's no way we could afford to buy both."

"But what about our new business?" asked Molly. "And the baby? Is now really a good time to invest in yet another business opportunity?"

"And could we honestly justify the expense?" Grace chimed in. "Our town is nowhere near big enough to support a hotel. It likely never will be again, revitalized or not."

"I don't think we should run it as a hotel. We should use it as a bed-and-breakfast. We'll keep the business model you two have already established; just open it up to more people. More people equals more money," he said as if it were a no-brainer. "We could also look into offering a few units to long-term renters. This town has a serious lack of rentals available."

"I feel like I'm intruding on what should really be a discussion between you guys," Grace said as she gathered her things to leave.

"This concerns you too, Grace," Grant said as he blocked her path to the exit.

"I have no money to contribute, have zero construction skills, and have no way to get a loan," she said as she skillfully weaved her way around him. "I also think you might have gone a little crazy. Anyway, I'm off to clean and try out more recipes. Good luck!"

She waved through the door as she made her way to her car. Out of curiosity, she took the long way home and drove by the old hotel. Stopping on the street, she stared up at the once grand hotel. It wasn't hard to imagine what it was like in its glory days. What was hard to imagine was bringing it back from the brink of death to something even remotely resembling its former glory. Still, if she tilted her head just right, she could almost catch a glimpse of Grant's vision.

***

It was eight o'clock, and Hunter still had yet to arrive. Nor had he called or texted. Still in the kitchen, where she had spent the day cooking enough food to feed an army, Grace continued making dish after dish. She was almost out of ingredients at this point, yet she couldn't stop herself. Her goal was to wait downstairs for Hunter to arrive without looking like she was waiting for him to arrive. Cooking was the only plan she could come up with to achieve that goal.

Fifteen minutes later, the doorbell finally rang. In order to appear unbothered, she took her time to answer the door. When she finally opened it, she was shocked to see her shell of a boyfriend standing on the other side. He was still as handsome as ever, but dark circles were under his eyes, and he looked like he hadn't slept or eaten in weeks.

Without saying a word, Grace backed up to make room for Hunter to walk through the door. She then closed and locked the door behind them. "I'm sure you're tired. Your room is ready for you upstairs. Same one as before." With that done, she returned to the kitchen, proud she'd managed to get through their first meeting without crying like a baby.

With shaky hands, she pulled her latest creation out of the oven. She was so intent on not dropping the hot pan she didn't notice he had followed her and was now standing directly behind her. When she turned around to grab another oven mitt, she almost had a heart attack when she came face to face with the man who had ghosted her and broken her heart. When she swayed a little to the right, he caught her and pulled her to his chest, wrapping his arms around her back.

She didn't want to admit how good it felt to be held in his arms, so she kept her body straight and refused to hug him back. After a moment, he chuckled and released her.

"I suppose I deserve your anger," he finally said. "I know I owe you an explanation. Can we talk?"

It was tempting to ignore him and give him a taste of what he had put her through. But while being petty can provide a sense of satisfaction, she ultimately decided against it. "Are you hungry?" she asked instead. "As you can see, I have a ton of food."

He glanced around the room. "I see that. Why do you have so much food? Are you expecting company?"

"No," she said with a shrug. "I've been working on recipes for the next round of guests. I could use another taste tester if you're interested?"

"I'm starving, so yes, I would love to be your guinea pig," he replied warily.

She shot him a look. "My cooking has improved immensely," she replied haughtily.

He held his hands up, palms out. "I'm sure it has. I'm looking forward to it," he quickly replied.

Grabbing a plate off the counter, she cut a piece of the coffee cake she had just made and placed it on the plate. She then piled a heaping spoonful of egg casserole, multiple pieces of bacon, and several mini quiches on the plate next to it. After handing it to him, she walked over to the table and sat down. She had waited an entire month to hear from him, and right now, all she wanted was an explanation.

"I owe you an apology," he stated. "The way I treated you was inexcusable, so I'm not even going to try." He took a couple of bites of his food. "Wow, this is really good," he said after he finished chewing.

Grace had never felt like a particularly patient person. She also lacked the experience and social skills to play the mind games that were prevalent among the dating crowd. "If you've changed your mind about having a relationship with me, please just tell me."

Hunter stopped chewing and stared at her. It took a lot of effort on her part not to read into his 'deer-in-the-headlights' expression. After a couple of minutes of silence, he ran his hands through his hair and sighed.

"I can see why you would think that. Honestly, I haven't changed my mind...but things for me have changed."

"Changed? In what way?" Her stomach tightened in apprehension. The moment she had dreaded had finally arrived; she could feel it in her bones.

"There are a lot of feelings to unpack. Too much for tonight. I know this isn't fair, but can we postpone this conversation until tomorrow? I promise I'll do my best to explain things then."

If he hadn't looked so exhausted and sad, she would have refused his request and demanded he explain everything then and there. But she had already waited a month; one more day wouldn't kill her. At least he was finally there. That was enough for now.

So she did her level best to be an adult, nodded in agreement, and then stood up to clear his empty plate. "You should go to bed. Everything is just as it was the last time you were here. If you need anything else, just let me know."

He stood up and came around to her side of the table. After an awkward couple of seconds, he pulled her into another hug. "Thank you, Grace. I really am happy to see you again."

Finally, giving in to the urge to hug him back, she quickly wrapped her arms around his waist and then stepped back. "Good night, Hunter."

"Good night, Grace."

She watched him walk out of the room. After weeks of alternating dreams and nightmares, the moment she had been waiting for had come and gone. There had been no declarations of love nor dramatic breakups. No tears of joy or sorrow. Just two people trying to navigate an awkward situation. So why did her heart still feel so broken?

-Days till Valentine's Day-

Fifteen

"Good morning, everyone!" Grace called out cheerfully. "Food is on the bar; help yourselves to as much as you like." Choosing to ignore the few skeptical looks between the non-believers, Grace continued to pour glasses of orange juice. After bringing them to the table and passing them out, she helped herself to a plate and sat down.

When she noticed everyone staring at her instead of eating, she put her fork down and stared back. "What?" she finally asked. "Y'all already ate or something?"

"No, dear, it's just, where did all this food come from?" asked Granny.

"I made it," replied Grace. Yes, she had a bad reputation in the kitchen, but this was starting to get ridiculous. People are capable of learning new skills, for heaven's sake.

"It's a lot of food," Molly grinned. "But it's delicious." She continued to shovel food into her mouth, the only one thus far to start eating.

"Thank you, Molly," Grace said, giving her a huge smile. "It's nice to see someone appreciate my cooking."

"Oh, I definitely appreciate it," she said between bites. "These mini quiches are to die for!"

One by one, they began to eat, hesitantly at first, but once they realized Molly wasn't just being nice, they started to dig in. Grace was more than a little offended but decided to ignore them. She was more interested in talking to Hunter than what her friends and family thought of her cooking skills.

When breakfast was over, Grant stood up and grabbed his coat. "I need to head into the office," he said as he put his coat on. "Hunter, are you coming with me?"

Hunter wiped his face with a napkin and then stood up as well. "Yes, I'm coming," he said as he shot Grace an apologetic look. "I've got a lot of catching up to do."

Grace started to protest but was cut off by Granny.

"You guys have a good day at work," she said cheerfully.

For the first time in her life, Grace was seriously annoyed with Granny. She would now be forced to wait the entire day to finally talk to Hunter. Although, if she didn't know better, she might think he was avoiding her. He could have easily told Grant he would meet him there later, yet he jumped at the chance to leave with him instead. This was getting ridiculous.

After the boys left, Grace and Molly got Granny and Gladys situated in Granny's room, then settled back down at the dining table.

"How did things go with Hunter last night?" Molly asked. "Did you get your answers?"

Grace shook her head, clearly annoyed. "He showed up acting as if nothing had happened, and when I wouldn't play along, apologized for ghosting me. When I asked for an explanation, he claimed to be tired and asked if we could talk today. As you can see," Grace waved her hand toward the door. "He left before we could talk."

Molly scrunched her nose. "Really? He gave zero explanation for the way he's been treating you?"

"I asked flat out if his feelings had changed, and while he denied it, he did claim that other things had changed. Or something like that..." she trailed off. "I have no idea what that even means. Is he only back for a couple of days or weeks? Or is he here for good? I only saw one suitcase last night, so the answer could be any of the above."

"I'm sorry. I didn't get to know him that well during Christmas, but from what I could tell, this just doesn't seem like him. Hopefully, he'll talk to you tonight."

"Hopefully. I deserve to know the truth, whatever it is." Grace's mind wandered off for a few minutes until she remembered what happened the day before. "Hey, how did things go with Grant after I left? Are you two seriously considering buying the old hotel?"

Molly looked at her thoughtfully over the rim of her tea cup. "I can see his vision," she said slowly. "But I admit I was also caught off guard."

"I just can't see how it's a viable business opportunity," said Grace. "Even though the building is old and needs repair, it's still a large, three-story brick building. They're going to want a lot of money for it. When you add in the extensive repairs, it could take decades for the property to pay itself back."

"All that is true," Molly agreed. "But if someone else buys it and competes with us, they could completely put us out of business."

"Unless the person that buys it is filthy stinking rich and can afford to hire a massive crew to do all the renovations, it will be years before they're ready to compete with us. I just can't see someone willing to take that risk for a bed-and-breakfast only open during holidays."

"There were a lot of people who saw how successful we were," Molly pointed out. "It's important to strike when the iron is hot, as they say."

"We were successful one time. That hardly qualifies us as a successful business venture. More importantly, we had to create a reason for people to come. Others have tried a regular bed-and-breakfast in the past. Each one failed due to lack of visitors."

Molly sighed. "I guess you're right. I just don't like the idea of someone else coming in and ruining our chance for success. I know how important this is to you."

Grace reached across the table and squeezed Molly's hand. "I appreciate that. This business is important to me, and I'm willing to do whatever it takes to protect it. I just can't see how this could benefit us."

"I hope you're right. Regardless, it will be weeks before the hotel is listed for sale, and, in the meantime, we have more pressing concerns to deal with."

"Such as?"

"Such as making sure that Amy over at 'A Gentle Touch' is onboard with our spa plan. Without her, it's not much of a 'spa experience'."

"Want to go back over there this morning and see if she's available to meet with us?"

"I think we should. I need to get this marketing campaign going as soon as possible, and she's the lynchpin holding me up."

"Say no more. I'll grab my coat, and we'll be on our way."

"Do you think she's open? Most businesses seem to be closed on Mondays around here."

"While that is true for most, there are some exceptions. Hopefully, she's one of them."

"I guess there's only one way to find out."

***

When they arrived at Amy's, she had just finished with a client.

"Perfect timing, ladies. What can I do for you?" she asked.

Amy was a lovely woman, petite in frame yet strong as an ox, likely from years of giving people massages. Married to the local CPA, she shared a building with her husband, each working out of a specific side.

"We're here to see if you would be interested in participating in the spa package we're putting together for our Valentine's Day guests," Molly replied.

"Oh? This is the first time I've heard about this. Is it going to be like the Christmas thing y'all did?"

"Not exactly. This time, we're targeting single people. We want it to feel like they're getting a luxury experience. Self-care and all that," Molly explained.

"And what would you like from me?"

"We want you to provide a massage. Then, they'll head to Lulu's to get their nails and hair done. After that, they'll head over to Chrissy's boutique, where they'll pick an outfit for the murder mystery dinner we're putting on that night."

"Both Chrissy and Lula will be offering wine and chocolate to sort of 'class things up,'" Grace added. "So if you can think of anything 'extra' to add to the package, it would really help us sell."

"I'll get paid for this, right?"

"Of course. In fact, all of this will be prepaid, as it will be included in the package. So we'll need prices as well," Molly responded.

"Hmm," Amy tapped her index finger against her chin as she thought. "What if I offered a fancy, personalized robe?" she wondered out loud. "Of course, that means I'll need names in advance. The sooner, the better. Also, I could make up a special, customized aromatherapy blend for each one. I already do that anyway, but they don't need to know that."

"All of that sounds great!" Molly assured her. "That should get them good and relaxed before heading to Lula's."

"Do you think I should offer wine?" asked Amy. "It doesn't fit with the ambiance here, but I don't want to be the odd man out, so to speak."

"How about a bottle of sparkling water, instead? This is more of a healthy place, so wine might feel out of place.

"I agree with Molly," said Grace. "You could throw in some pre-packaged health food to go with the water while they wait. Like a bag of trail mix or nuts?"

Molly nodded. "That could work. Just a little something extra that feels special but doesn't detract from the actual service you're offering. After all, the massage is the important part."

"But isn't the same true for the other services?" she asked.

"Kind of," said Molly. "A massage is more...personal. Here, we want them to focus on relaxing, not the drink in their hand."

Amy nodded as she processed that bit of information. "That sounds good to me. I can email you a price in a couple of hours if that will work?"

"That would be perfect," Molly said with a smile. She held out her hand for Amy to shake. "It's been a pleasure doing business with you."

Amy shook her hand. "Likewise. I look forward to doing more business with you in the future."

Molly handed Amy a business card, presumably with her contact information, and then she and Grace returned to the car. "That went well," said Molly.

"Yes, it did. The people around here sure come up with a lot of good ideas. It's a shame they've never been able to do something like this before."

"In my experience, people tend to be pretty creative; they just need an outlet," Molly said, her brow raised. "Something we have been able to provide."

"Why do I get the feeling that was also directed at me?"

"Because it was. You've already proven you're so much more capable than you ever thought possible.

All that's left for you to do now is believe it."

"I'm getting there, but it takes time to undo years of self-deprecating beliefs."

"That's an interesting way of saying it takes time to build up low self-esteem," Molly smiled to soften her somewhat harsh words. "I can see you're getting better, and I'm proud of you. I just thought you could use a little reminder now and then."

"Thanks...I think."

They pulled up to Grace's house, and she got ready to exit the car. She was a little jealous that Molly had a new job to go to while she was stuck spending her day taking care of Granny and Gladys. Not that she minded taking care of them; she just wished she had a purpose beyond caring for the house and its inhabitants.

Soon, there would be more guests to entertain and cook for. She would just have to be content with what she had and learn to love the downtime. In the meantime, she had plenty of new recipes to try. Who knew there were so many options for breakfast out there!

-Days till Valentine's Day-

Fourteen

Grace awoke in a foul mood. Hunter had stayed out so late the night before she ended up with no choice but to go to bed without talking to him. He was definitely avoiding her, which made him a coward in her book, a coward and a jerk. Right before he left for New York, he had kissed her passionately, promised to call her every day, and said he would hurry back. Instead, he had ghosted her almost immediately, taken twice as long to return, and was now stringing her along for who knows what reason.

One of the things she recently learned about herself was that she was the kind of person who liked to confront her problems head-on. She didn't like wasting time worrying about things and would prefer to look for solutions rather than pretend the problem didn't exist. Hunter was apparently the opposite type of person. While she felt it was good to find this out now, she needed to figure out how to navigate these choppy waters. Should she try to force him to talk when he wasn't ready? Or should she completely ignore her own needs and give him the space he obviously wanted? Suddenly, single life didn't seem so bad.

She continued to mull over her options while dressed, but sadly, no solution popped into her head. When she left her room, she paused in front of his door to see if she could hear him up and about. When she did, she made a decision. He didn't have to give her answers about their relationship, but he did have to at least tell her his plans for living there. With that decision made, she decided to wait in front of his door and confront him as soon as he opened it.

Thankfully, she didn't have to wait long for him to appear. A few minutes later, he opened the door, saw her standing there with her arms crossed, and jumped almost a foot in the air. It would have been funny if she wasn't so mad.

"Grace, oh my gosh," he exclaimed, his hand flying to his chest. "You nearly gave me a heart attack. What are you doing?"

"Waiting for you. It seems this is the only way I can get you to talk to me."

He stared at her for a few seconds, clearly at a loss for words. Finally, he sighed and ran a hand through his hair. "I'm sorry—"

Grace held up her hand. "Please spare me your excuses and half-hearted apologies," she interrupted. "You don't want to talk, fine. But at the very least, I have a right to know your plans regarding living in this house. In case you forgot, we agreed you would pay rent. I need to know if you will break that agreement so I can plan accordingly."

"Honestly, I don't know. I know that's unfair, but it's the best I can do right now."

Grace took a couple of steps forward and got right in his face, her anger pushed to a limit it had never before reached. "Since you've been gone, Gladys broke her hip, leaving me to deal with two elderly women, both of whom are incapable of taking care of their most basic needs without help. Inflation has caused food and gas prices to soar, and I had to spend thousands of dollars to replace our broken furnace. You already know money is tight around here, so, quite frankly, your best isn't good enough."

"I had no idea—" he started to say.

"You had no idea because you refused to answer or return my calls," she interrupted again. "Look, I have no idea what's going on with you because you've decided to shut me out," she drawled. "But this isn't the 'Hunter Show'. Your actions affect a lot of other people. I expect an answer by the end of the week, which is way more time than you deserve."

Before he could respond, she turned on her heel, walked down the stairs, and went to the kitchen to make breakfast. Even though she was angry, there were still six people to feed, and she would not become a hypocrite and shirk her duties like she had just accused him of doing. Molly, Grant, Gladys, and Granny were already seated at the table when she arrived, each attempting to look like they hadn't just been eavesdropping.

Unable to force even the slightest smile, she nodded in their direction and continued into the kitchen to start the coffee. Making more noise than was necessary, she began pulling containers out of the fridge to reheat for their breakfast. They had barely made a dent in the food she had made over the last couple of days, which was actually a good thing when she thought about it. Knowing how long food would last before it started to taste...old would be very helpful. It would also be beneficial to know which types of food were still acceptable after they were reheated versus which ones were better fresh. Better to find these things out now than when her guests arrived.

As she emptied containers into the pans heating on the stove, she felt a hand on her shoulder.

"Are you okay?" Molly whispered.

That was a good question. Was she okay? She couldn't remember the last time she had confronted someone like that. In fact, she might have never been in a fight like that before. She was upset, angry, embarrassed to have been overheard by everyone else, yet she was also...proud? Yes, she was definitely proud. Proud, she finally stood up for herself. Proud for letting him know that his behavior was unacceptable, she wouldn't just sit back and take it.

Turning to look at Molly, she gave a real, genuine smile. "Yeah, I'm okay."

Molly studied her for a couple of seconds, then smiled back. "Good, anything I can do to help? With breakfast or...anything else?"

"Breakfast is under control, but I could use some help serving the coffee. Also, we need to finalize our plans so we can start advertising. Are you available to work on that this morning?"

Molly grabbed mugs out of the cupboard and filled them with coffee. "I have as much time as you need."

"Great, we can get started after breakfast."

Grace made enough for six people, but Hunter never showed up. Halfway through breakfast, they heard the front door open and close, but no one said anything. By that point, her anger had turned to hurt. A large part of her had hoped her words would spur him to action. Instead, if his leaving without a word was any indication, she had only pushed him further away. She had lost him, although maybe she had never really had him.

***

"Okay," Grace said by way of starting their unofficial meeting. "We plan on the guests arriving Friday night, so I'm thinking we could set out a buffet-style dinner they could help themselves to whenever they want since it's likely they'll be arriving at different times,"

"I would also put out some wine," Molly mused out loud as she typed notes on her laptop. "Not saying all single people love to drink, but I feel like it might be expected for this type of event."

Grace nodded along as she consulted her own hand-written notes. "Saturday has already been covered, which brings us to Sunday." She thought about it for a few minutes. Sundays were hard days to plan for. Many people spent the morning at church, businesses were closed, at least in Winterwood, and most considered it a day of rest. "I guess we could do another horse and carriage ride?"

"We could, but I don't think it will have the same amount of charm as last time. Saturday will be such a busy day; what if we have a lazy day instead?"

"What do you mean? Everyone just hangs out in their rooms?" Grace wasn't sure about that idea. Some might like it, but others could end up bored.

"That is one option, but there are plenty of other things we could offer instead. Such as board games, a cooking lesson, puzzles, arts and crafts projects..." she trailed off, either because she was out of ideas or because she figured she'd made her point.

"That could work. We should have potential guests choose a couple of options when they book, and then we can plan on offering the most popular ones.

"Sounds good," Molly replied, typing away on her keyboard. "That brings us to Monday. Any thoughts?"

Christmas had been so much easier to plan. There seemed to be a never-ending supply of ideas to keep people entertained around the happiest time of the year, she thought as she rolled her eyes. Monday was a work day, and people rarely took time off from work around Valentine's Day, so it was unlikely they could do anything that would draw a crowd from the neighboring towns.

"Oh! I just had an idea," Grace announced excitedly. "Beverly, one of the ladies at the library, does pottery. What if we get her to teach a pottery class? This way, the guests would have something they could take home with them, too."

Molly tilted her head to the side as she thought about it. "I think that sounds like a great idea. Do you think Beverly would agree to teach the class?"

"I don't see why she wouldn't; she loves pottery. But just to be safe, I'll call her and ask."

Grace went into the kitchen to start lunch as she called down to the library. Time sure did fly when she wasn't anxiously watching the clock. As she had predicted, Beverly jumped at the chance to give the guests a pottery lesson. They would have to go to her shop since all her supplies, including her pottery wheels and kiln, were kept there, but that wasn't a big deal.

She relayed the news to Molly as she fixed trays for Granny and Gladys. "It looks like we have everything set. Is it time to start advertising?"

"Yep, I'm just putting the finishing touches on my campaign. I'm going to run ads on a few of my social media accounts."

"The same ones as last time?"

"No, since we're trying to reach a different crowd, I'll use ones geared more toward young professionals. I have a feeling it won't take long to garner some interest, especially since I'm calling this my anti-Valentine's Day campaign. We might even go viral," she said excitedly.

Grace shook her head. Until recently, she hadn't had a single social media account. She only had one now to look up relatives for her previous guest. All of this 'viral' stuff went entirely over her head. Another reason to be grateful for Molly, who had her pulse on all the latest and greatest social media had to offer.

"I guess I'll just have to trust you," she finally responded. "We only need four people this time, so hopefully, the spots will fill up just as fast as last time."

"Don't worry, Grace, I have a good feeling about this."

Grace smiled, but it didn't quite reach her eyes. No matter how hard she tried, she couldn't get excited about this newest adventure. What had started as a one-time thing to bring her granny out of depression had turned into a full-time job. Grace felt she already had several full-time jobs since she spent most of her time caring for Granny and Gladys. Adding four extra people on top was overwhelming, to say the least. But they needed the money, so she'd do what she had to do.

-Days till Valentine's Day-

Thirteen

"We have problems," Grace announced as she walked into the dining room Wednesday morning. "Lots and lots of problems."

"What's wrong?" Molly asked, looking up from her laptop screen.

"Both Bea and Addie have now fully canceled on providing meals for our guests' stay, and Mayor Allen just informed me we need a liquor license for both the murder mystery dinner and the Valentine's Day mixer."

"Oh, those are definitely problems," Molly said as she closed her laptop and gave Grace her full attention. "Let's start with the food. I thought Bea and Addie were happy to have the business?"

"They were until they both got so busy they no longer had time for us," Grace crinkled her nose. "Apparently, multiple moms have ordered cookies and cupcakes for their kids' Valentine's Day parties at school. Add in her regular business, special orders, and the catering for the two big events we're throwing; she just doesn't have time. The same goes for Addie." Grace sighed as she paced in front of the table.

There were a couple of other restaurants in town, but as much as she hated to say it, neither produced the same food quality as Addie and Bea. Since she was charging her guests good money for the food, she needed to be careful that it met their standards, especially since the nearest chain restaurant was a good forty-five minutes away. The last thing she needed was guests leaving bad reviews based on the food.

"I guess you'll just have to do the cooking," Molly said with a shrug. "Your cooking skills have vastly improved over the last few days; I have no doubt you can do it. Besides, this just means money that would have gone to them will now go to you. That could be considered a win."

"I still have to buy the ingredients, not to mention all the time it will take to cook three meals a day for ten people," Grace sighed again at the thought. "I've only mastered breakfast. I'm not sure there's enough time to master dinner and desserts."

"Keep the menu simple, offer comfort-style food, and focus on flavor. If you can master those three things, you'll do just fine," Grant interjected from behind the newspaper he was reading. "As for the liquor license, go talk to the bar owners. If you partner with them, they can supply the license, the alcohol, and the staff to serve it."

Grace stared at the back of the newspaper. It was like talking to the man behind the curtain; only this one solved all her problems in the blink of an eye. "Thanks, Grant. I will take care of that first thing after breakfast."

"You'll need to wait till this afternoon." He folded the newspaper in half and placed it on the table before him. "Most bars open late and close late. So you're not likely to find the owner in till late this afternoon."

"Okayyy," Grace drawled. "I'll take care of it first thing this afternoon, then. Anyway, thanks again. You've been a big help."

"Anytime," he said with a grin. "Now, if you'll excuse me," he said as he got up. "I need to get to work." He kissed Molly on the cheek and headed for the front door.

"But I haven't served breakfast yet," Grace called after him as he shut the door.

"Don't worry about him; I already served breakfast to the group," said Molly. "I got Granny and Gladys settled too.

"Oh," Grace said as she slumped down in a chair. "Thanks."

"Any more problems we need to solve?"

Grace shook her head. She wasn't sure why, but she felt a little defeated. Or maybe she was just tired? Ever since Hunter returned, she'd been getting little to no sleep. It had made her groggy, grumpy, and put her on edge. Now that she had to add personal chef to her resume, she could add overwhelmed, anxious, and panicked to her list.

"Don't look so sad, I have great news!" Molly announced cheerfully.

At that, Grace perked up a little. "What news? Did we win the lottery?"

"No, silly, even better."

"What could be better than winning the lottery?"

"Rebekah Rutherford has booked one of our packages!" Molly exclaimed, practically bouncing up and down with excitement.

"Who's that?"

Molly rolled her eyes and sighed dramatically. "I keep forgetting how anti-social you are. Rebekah Rutherford is a Socialite from New York."

"I don't understand. You're from Boston, so how do you know a woman from New York?"

"I don't 'know her' know her, silly. She has a HUGE following on Instagram. I'm talking over a million followers. If she makes even one post about our bed-and-breakfast, we'll never have to worry about booking guests again."

"Doesn't that make the opposite true as well? If she makes even one negative post, we'll never book another guest again?"

"I suppose, but we don't need to worry about that. There's no reason for her to say anything negative about us."

"I don't know, Molly. I have zero experience in this area, but from everything I have ever read about 'influencers,' they tend to be demanding and hard to please. Are you sure this is a good idea?"

"It doesn't matter whether it's a good idea. We can't tell her no, especially after I've already accepted her request."

"What request?" Grace asked nervously. All of a sudden, she had a strange feeling in her gut. You know, the kind you get when something terrible is about to happen?

"She asked if she could come a week early, and I said yes. She has a travel blog and is currently between locations. Don't worry, though," Molly added quickly when she saw the look on Grace's face. "I made sure to charge her plenty of money to make it worth your while."

"You agreed to let her come an entire week early without asking me first? How could you do that to me?"

"It just kind of happened. We were on the phone, and I was so excited I got carried away. I'm sorry; I truly thought you'd be as thrilled as I am."

The only thing that saved Molly from Grace's new-found temper was that she at least had the decency to look apologetic. The fact she was pregnant, and Grace didn't want to risk upsetting her didn't hurt either. Today was Wednesday, which meant Grace had precisely two days to go from being the world's worst cook to something at least passable. Worse than that, she was expected to cook for a world-traveling socialite influencer. Everything about that sentence screamed rich, entitled, demanding snob. Although, maybe she was just being judgmental and harsh. Time will tell.

***

Grace had planned to make a menu, starting with the dinner on the Friday before Valentine's Day. She would then spend the next week and a half practicing cooking her chosen menu items. Since things had now changed, that plan was out the window. Instead, she spent hours pouring over menus from every five-star restaurant she could find. When she came across an item she thought she had a reasonable chance of success making, she added it to her list.

Once the list was complete, she switched to watching YouTube videos of people demonstrating how to make the food in question. By the time she was ready to meet the bartender, she had a binder the size of a phone book full of recipes with a copious amount of notes on how to make them. She might fail, but at this point, she would die trying.

Before she left, she checked on Granny and Gladys. They were all set to watch Jeopardy, a show they loved almost as much as Wheel of Fortune. Grace hated to leave them, but they both assured her they could survive an hour without her. Before Gladys had broken her hip, she had been Grace's go-to sitter for Granny. Having someone who could watch over Granny without making her feel like a child had been a relief. Now Gladys was in the same boat, and Grace had no one to turn to for help. Well, she now had Grant and Molly, but they were both busy at work.

Determined to make this visit as quick as possible, Grace drove the five blocks to the bar instead of walking. It would have been nice to get out and get some exercise, but practicality won out in the end. When she got to the bar, she parked on the street in front and hurried to the door. The sign said the bar didn't open until five, but a quick push on the door showed it was unlocked, so she took a chance and went in.

"Hello?" she called out in the semi-dark room. She had lived in Winterwood for twenty years and been of legal drinking age for at least four, yet had never been inside the bar before. It was a medium-sized space. There were a couple of pool tables along the right side of the wall, a handful of tables and chairs in the middle of the room, and a bar lined with bar stools that ran the entire left side. It had a dark and dingy feel, but that might result from most of the lights being off and only one large window letting light through.

"Is someone here?" called a voice from somewhere far away.

Before she answered, she stepped further into the room and saw a door in the back behind the bar. It was most likely the storeroom where they kept all the alcohol.

"Hello?" the voice called out again. A few seconds later, a man came through the door, wiping his hands on a rag. When he spotted her, he stopped walking. "Well, hello there, I thought I heard a voice. We're closed right now, but if you come back in an hour, I'll make sure to get you taken care of."

Grace was not one to fawn over men. Yes, she could recognize a handsome man when she saw one; hello, Hunter, but she usually had no problem continuing on with her business. This man, however, took her breath away. He was tall and wore low-slung jeans, a tight-fitting t-shirt that showed off his tattooed biceps, and a cowboy hat. It would not be an exaggeration to say he looked like he had just stepped out of an ad for a Levi's campaign. Or off a ranch, where he spent the day riding horses and herding cattle.

When she didn't respond, he raised his brow. "Everything okay, darlin'?"

Shaking her head, she finally recovered her voice. "I'm sorry, I didn't mean to intrude. I'm looking for Ted. Do you know when he'll be back?"

"Last I heard, Ted's on a beach somewhere in Mexico. So, I'm guessing it won't be any time soon."

"What? Ted's in Mexico?" This was just great. What was she supposed to do now? She had an event that was supposed to take place in just over a week, and the one man who could solve her problem was in Mexico. If she didn't have bad luck, she would have no luck at all.

"Is there something I can help you with?" Mr. Too Sexy for his own good asked.

Grace shook her head. "Not unless you're willing and able to authorize using the bar's liquor license for the event I'm putting on next Saturday night."

"I can help with that. Is this the big murder mystery dinner everyone keeps talking about?"

Grace looked up at him in surprise. "You've heard about that?"

"Sure have," he said, nodding his head. "It's the talk of the town. Almost everyone I've talked to plans to attend."

"Oh! Well, that's a relief. I was worried we might not sell any tickets. Anyway, I just discovered I can't provide alcohol without a license, so I was hoping you might be willing to partner with me for the event. Well, this one and the one we're hosting on the following Tuesday."

"And what would this partnership look like?" he drawled.

It just figured his voice would match his looks. There wasn't a celebrity she could think of that could come anywhere close to matching his looks and charm. "Um," she said, clearing her throat nervously. "There will be food stations around town, so I need servers to serve wine and beer at each station. The first drink, which we will pay for, is included in the ticket price. All additional drinks will be paid for by the customer."

"It sounds like this might be worth closing the bar for a night. I'm Cole, by the way," he said, extending his hand. "If we're going to be partners, it might be best to know who we're partnering with."

"I'm Grace," she said as she shook his hand, little jolts of electricity pulsating throughout her arm.

He gave her a look that made it more than a little clear he knew exactly what kind of effect he was having on her. "You must be the Grace responsible for all the Christmas hoopla."

"I'm not sure I would call it 'hoopla,'" she said, making finger quotes on the word hoopla. "But yes, that would be me."

"Didn't mean to offend you, just didn't know what to call it," he said with a smile. "Well, Miss Grace, I reckon we have ourselves a deal."

"Are you sure Ted won't mind? I don't want to get anyone in trouble."

"Ted sold me this bar last November. So, yes, I'm sure he won't mind."

Grace nodded, unable to think of anything else to say. "Okay, well, thank you. I'll contact you as soon as we have all the details."

"Sounds good, and if you ever want that drink, you know where to find me."

He said the last part in such a way it almost sounded like an invitation to something much more than a drink. But that was crazy and likely just her imagination and wounded pride over being dumped by Hunter talking. A man like Cole would never in a million years be interested in someone like her. And after everything that happened with Hunter, it would be wise of her not to waste her time drooling over men who were that far out of her league. The heart could only break so many times.

-Days till Valentine's Day-

Twelve

Thursday afternoon found Grace in the kitchen, panicking over her third batch of ruined alfredo sauce. No matter what she did, she just couldn't keep her sauce from sticking to the bottom of the pan and burning. Which was terrible since this was supposed to be her go-to meal for easy, tasty, comfort-style food. Unsure of what to do next, she returned to the giant binder and tried to find an easier recipe.

"Something smells...interesting," said Hunter as he walked into the kitchen.

Startled by the unexpected intrusion, Grace dropped her binder, the contents spilling all over the floor. She bent down to pick them up and almost bumped heads with Hunter, who had come around the counter to help. "Sorry," she said as she straightened up and stepped back. "I didn't think anyone else was here right now."

She really meant she didn't expect him to be there. Ever since their confrontation the other day, he had continued to avoid her, skipping breakfast and dinner and staying out way past bedtime. His behavior was so unlike the man she knew at Christmas she almost wondered if he had a twin he had switched places with when he went back to New York.

"I didn't mean to startle you," he said quietly. "I was hoping we could talk for a few minutes."

Grace raised her brow in question, too excited to respond with words. Would she finally get the answers she so desperately craved? He reached into his pocket and pulled out a white envelope. When he handed it to her, she took it, confused and caught off guard. "What's this?" she asked.

"It's a check for the rent money I owe you. There's enough to cover January through March. I can't promise to stay beyond that, but it will at least cover my time here."

"You weren't here in January," Grace said, unable to keep the disappointment from her voice. While the money was appreciated, this was not the conversation she had hoped to have.

"I know, but I said I'd be. It's not your fault things changed on my end."

"Are you ready to finally tell me what these changes are?" she asked hopefully.

Hunter shook his head, his face immediately changed to what she thought of as his professional mask. "I understand everyone wants answers, but at this time, I have none to give. You'll just have to be patient a little longer."

"And if I don't want to?" she asked. "Be patient," she clarified when he looked confused. "I don't understand why you can't just be honest with me?"

"Telling you I need time is my way of being honest. And if you don't want to be patient, I guess your only option is to kick me out. Other than that, I don't know what to tell you."

That was a really crummy thing to say, and she was tempted to take him up on his offer. But practicality and the needs of her family won out in the end. She would have to return his rent check if she kicked him out. She hadn't been kidding when she said she needed money. "Fine, take all the time you need," she finally responded.

At that, she turned her back to him and continued looking for recipes. When she heard his footsteps retreating down the hall, she looked up just in time to hear the front door open and close again. Just like that, he was gone; the only evidence he had been there in the first place was the white envelope she had placed on the counter. At least he had honored her demand to inform her of his plans.

With a heavy sigh, she picked up the binder and carried it to the table so she could sit down. She wasn't sure what was worse: being ghosted by a man who lived hundreds of miles away or ghosted by a man who lived in the same house. After a few minutes of thought, she decided it was definitely worse to live with the guy. Knowing he was only a few feet away, yet still chose to ignore her, was not only painful, she had lost the ability to fool herself into thinking he was just busy.

Regardless of all the drama she was facing, she still had an inn to run and a guest to prepare for. A guest who literally had the power to make or break her business. If that didn't scream 'stress,' she didn't know what did. So, it was time to put her big-girl panties on and get to work. After all, this food wasn't going to cook itself.

***

Hunter surprised everyone by showing up for dinner that night. It was the first time he had done so since he returned from New York, and Grace had foolishly allowed herself to hope it was a sign things might return to normal. Instead, an awkward and somewhat tense conversation followed, where everyone tried to ignore the elephant in the room. Unsurprisingly, he beat a hasty retreat to his room as soon as he deemed it socially acceptable.

Unable to spend another stressful night cooped up in the house thinking about him, Grace left Granny and Gladys in Molly's capable hands and went out. It was uncharacteristically nice for an evening in February, so Grace decided to go down to the pond and walk around. A little fresh air and what remained of the sunlight would do wonders for her mood.

A couple of laps into her walk, she saw a strange-looking vehicle approaching from the field behind the park. A little concerned about being caught out alone by a stranger, she quickly turned toward her car when she heard the stranger call her name. Turning back around, she saw Cole waving at her, the world's biggest dog in the seat beside him.

Not wanting to be rude, especially to the man who had just saved her behind, she waited for him to close the distance. "Hey," she said when he arrived. "What are you doing out here? And what's this vehicle you're driving?"

"It's a mule," he said with a laugh. "It's like a golf cart for farmers," he elaborated when she gave him a confused look. "We use them to carry feed and tools when doing farm chores, which I just finished doing."

"Oh," she said as realization dawned on her. "You must own the farm behind the park."

"Yes, ma'am," he grinned.

"And who is this handsome fellow?" she asked as she pet the gigantic dog's head. A loud laugh escaped when he turned and licked her face with his equally giant tongue.

"This big guy is Max, he's a bullmastiff."

"He's huge," Grace said with a laugh. "I bet he's as tall as you when he stands up on his hind legs."

"You're not wrong," he said. "He's a great farm dog, though. Keeps the predators at bay." Cole gave the dog a loving pat on his back, his love for the animal written on his handsome face. "So, what brings you out tonight?" he asked, facing her again.

Grace shrugged. "Just out for a walk. It's not too often we see weather like this, this time of year."

"True," Cole nodded. "How are things going with your mystery dinner? You got those details worked out yet?"

"I'm still finalizing them, but I hope to get them to you in the next few days. We're still working out which shops will be involved and where the best places to host the food stations will be." She felt a strong need to defend herself, as if he accused her of not doing her job.

"No worries," he shrugged. "I'm just curious to see how it will work out. I'm pretty new to this bar-ownership thing. This will be my first time participating in something like this."

Now, she felt stupid for jumping to conclusions. "In all honesty, I'm pretty new to all of this, too. Christmas was the first time I opened my home as a bed-and-breakfast, and I had planned for it to be a one-time-only kind of thing. These events require much more planning and coordinating than I had anticipated."

"Ah, that explains why you didn't know about the liquor license." He was silent for a minute as if thinking about something. "Out of curiosity, what made you do this again?"

"I guess the same reason people do anything...money."

When he stared at her instead of responding, she got nervous, and when she got nervous, she tended to start rambling. "My Granny is sick; her friend Gladys fell and broke her hip, taxes are sky high, and when you add in the cost of food and gas due to continuously rising inflation..." she stopped to take a breath. "Simply put, we need more money to live now." She felt her cheeks redden in embarrassment and hoped it was now dark enough that he couldn't tell.

"I could always use another bartender," he finally offered.

'Th-thank you," she stammered. "But I have zero knowledge of how to bar-tend, and even if I did, Granny needs a full-time caretaker. Any money I made outside the home would just go to the caretaker I would have to hire to take my place."

"Sounds like you're doing your best with the cards you've been dealt. I have a lot of respect for that," he said as he tipped his cowboy hat.

It didn't seem possible, but she was sure her cheeks reddened even more. No one had ever said they respected her before. She was pretty sure it was the best compliment she had ever received. "Thank you, that means a lot to me."

She stood there momentarily, trying to think of something else to say. When nothing came to mind, she decided to excuse herself and go home. "I guess I should let you get back to work."

"It was nice seeing you again, Miss Grace. My offer for that drink still stands; come in anytime."

"I just might take you up on that sometime," she winked at him and then turned around, horrified at how shamelessly she had just flirted with him. The sound of his deep chuckle as he started the mule and drove away only caused more embarrassment.

What is with her all of a sudden? She spent the first twenty-five years of her life practically living like a monk, and now, in the span of a few months, she's taken to flirting with every guy she met. Next thing you know, she'll be setting up accounts on dating sites.

Just like you shouldn't go grocery shopping when you're hungry, you shouldn't talk to men when you're lonely. It messes with your head. A lesson she should have already learned if Hunter was any indication. Oh well, a little flirting never hurt anyone. Right?

-Days till Valentine's Day-

Eleven

The moment Grace had been dreading finally arrived; Rebekah Rutherford was now standing in her living room, looking every inch the New York socialite Grace had imagined her to be. There was an air of sophistication about her Grace believed one could only be born with. They were close in age, yet so far apart in every other way it was almost like they were a different species. If this were a movie, Grace would play the part of the servant while Rebekah would be royalty.

Unfortunately, or fortunately, depending on your view, Rebekah had been nothing but kind, enthusiastically exclaiming over the inn and its charming quaintness every time Grace showed her a new room. For some reason, likely jealousy, Grace wanted to hate her, but she was making that very difficult by being so nice. Her ungracious thoughts and opinions about a woman she had just met were nothing short of shameful.

"Oh!" Rebekah exclaimed. "I just texted my boyfriend to tell him I'm here, and he's on his way to see me. Do you mind if we finish the tour later? I would like to freshen up before he gets here."

"Not at all; we were pretty much finished anyway," Grace replied, confused by the revelation of a boyfriend. Didn't Rebekah book the Valentine's Day package for singles? It didn't make sense she would do that if she had a boyfriend. "Um, is he planning on staying here with you?"

Rebekah had already reached the door to the foyer but paused to respond. Before she could, Hunter came running into the room, a panicked look on his face.

"Oh my gosh!" Rebekah squealed as she threw her arms around Hunter. "I'm so glad to see you. I've missed you so much!"

Grace watched in stunned silence as Hunter wrapped his arms around Rebekah, a miserable and somewhat resigned expression on his otherwise handsome face. She wanted to say something cutting and sarcastic. Something that would convey her hurt, anger, and betrayal, but no words would come. Instead, she stood there and watched as another woman hugged the man who was supposed to be her boyfriend. Awkward did not begin to describe the scene unfolding in front of her.

Rebekah let go and turned to Grace. "Looks like I was too late. This guy must have been so excited to see me he rushed home," she said as she patted his chest. "I guess this answers your question, too, right?"

"Um, what question is that?" Grace asked, confused thoughts swirling through her head.

"You asked if my boyfriend was planning to stay with me. Obviously, he's already staying here, so..." Rebekah trailed off, her expression tinged with annoyance at explaining the obvious.

Grace nodded and tried to smile, though she imagined it came out more of a grimace. "Right, of course. You'll have to forgive me; it's just, you booked our Valentine's Day package for single people. I'm a little caught off guard by you having a boyfriend."

It was Rebekah's turn to look confused, making her look more adorable. "I booked what?"

"The Valentine's Day package," Grace replied slowly. "The one we were advertising when you called and talked to my partner, Molly?"

She shook her head. "No, I have no idea what you're talking about. I called to book a room to spend time with Hunter."

"Oh," Grace replied, unsure of what to do now. "So, you booked the room expecting this to be more like a regular bed-and-breakfast?"

"Yes," Rebekah drawled out the word as if Grace lacked comprehension skills.

"I think the confusion is coming from the fact Grace only opens the bed-and-breakfast up for holiday events," Hunter said, finally speaking up after minutes of silently watching their conversation.

"Huh, the woman I spoke to on the phone didn't mention anything about that. This isn't going to be a problem, is it?"

The way she asked made it sound like more of a statement than a question. Grace knew better than to antagonize a paying guest, so she smiled as best as she could and reassured the woman. "Of course not; I just want to ensure our little inn lives up to your expectations. Since you booked the package, even if unintentionally, you are still entitled to attend the events we'll be hosting starting next Friday night. If you want to, that is."

"I'm sure Hunter and I will have our own plans, but I'll keep that in mind," she said politely. "I don't mean to be rude, but if you'll excuse us, I've come a long way, and I'd like to spend some alone time with my man."

Grace did, in fact, mind, but unless she wanted to make a scene, there was nothing she could do. "Of course, just let me know if you need anything."

"We would love a bottle of wine and a charcuterie board," she called over her shoulder as they left the room. "And some chocolate-covered strawberries if you have any. I've always thought those were so romantic, don't you agree, Hunter?"

Hunter mumbled something in response, then gently urged Rebekah up the stairs. It took Grace everything she had not to throw up as she listened to Rebekah squeal and giggle at Hunter's attention. This must be the change he had been referring to. The coward hadn't even had the decency to officially break up with her.

With more force than necessary, Grace made the requested charcuterie board and chocolate-covered strawberries. It wasn't until she almost cut her finger off that she finally stopped and took a step back to calm down. No man was worth injuring herself over, especially one who was as big a creep as Hunter now appeared to be.

When the board was finished, she took it upstairs, set it on the table outside Rebekah's door, knocked once, then ran back downstairs so she wouldn't have to see the love-birds again. Unable to stomach the thought of spending the rest of the night in the same house as them, she grabbed her purse and keys, sent a quick text to Molly asking her to take care of Granny and Gladys, and left.

***

Grace wasn't sure how she ended up parked in front of Ted's, which, upon closer inspection, now said Cole's, but she decided to go with it. She had never gotten drunk before, but if there was ever an occasion that warranted it, she figured this was it. A quick glance at her phone showed several missed calls and texts from Molly. Grace had zero desire to talk to the woman responsible for bringing Re-bekah to town, so she tossed her phone into the glove box and went inside.

The bar was a lot more crowded than she had expected. Yes, it was a Friday night, and yes, this was a small town with zero options for entertainment, but she still hadn't expected this many people. It looked like half the town was out to bear witness to her fall from grace.

After smiling and waving at a few familiar faces, she made her way to the end of the bar closest to the door. There were a couple of empty stools in that corner, and the lighting was dim, perfect for someone who planned to drown her sorrows. When she sat down, she looked around for the bartender and managed to spot Cole at the same time he saw her.

"Grace!" he exclaimed with a huge grin. "Finally decided to take me up on that drink, huh?"

"Looks that way," she responded sarcastically, immediately wincing when she saw the look on his face. "Sorry, I'm having a bad day."

"Okay, what can I get for you?"

"I don't know. Something fruity?"

"Never been in a bar before, have you?"

She shook her head in embarrassment. "I guess it's that obvious?"

"Maybe a little," he said with a smile. "But don't worry about it; I have just the thing." He walked away for a couple of minutes, presumably to make her drink. She tried to watch him, but he disappeared into the back room, leaving her alone in her dim little corner.

He reappeared a few minutes later with a glass full of orange-colored liquid, which he handed her. After taking a small sip, she looked up at him with narrowed eyes. "Did you just bring me a glass of orange juice?"

"It's called a screwdriver," he said with a laugh. "Relax, Grace, it's orange juice mixed with vodka. We don't normally serve cocktails here, so that's the closest you're going to get to 'something fruity,'" he said, making little air quotes with his fingers. "You must be having a terrible day; want to tell me about it?"

She winced at his words. He had been nothing but friendly and accommodating, and she was being a big jerk. "My boyfriend's new girlfriend just checked into my bed and breakfast."

"Ouch!" he said with a wince. "I take it you didn't know about this new woman?"

Grace took a deep breath and let it out slowly. "Looking back, I suppose the signs were there. I guess I just didn't want to see them." After she finished her sentence, she took a long sip of her drink. It had a strange taste, but she was sure she could grow to like it.

"I think you might need to slow down there, darlin'," he said as he pulled her glass back. "It will go straight to your head, especially if you haven't eaten?"

Grace didn't appreciate him telling her what to do, so she slid her glass back in front of her while giving him an 'I dare you to touch it again' look. "No, I haven't eaten. I was too upset to eat after I discovered I'm going to spend the next week and a half living with my ex and the woman he didn't even have the decency to properly dump me for."

Cole took a step back and held his hands up in surrender. "I'll go get you some wings and another drink."

Grace sighed at his retreating back. She hated the way she was acting but couldn't seem to make herself stop. Why she felt the need to treat him this way was beyond her comprehension. At some point, she would have to do some serious self-reflection.

He was gone long enough for her to finish her drink and properly chastise herself. "Thank you," she said when he placed the food and drink before her. "I really am sorry.

I'm being a huge jerk, and you definitely don't deserve to be treated that way."

Cole reached over and took her hand. "It's okay; I know it's just your hurt talking. You want to tell me what happened? From the beginning? It might help to get it all out," he said sympathetically.

She wasn't sure she was capable of forming words with his hand wrapped around hers and felt both grateful and bereft when he let go. After taking a deep breath to calm her nerves, she told him the story of how she and Hunter had gotten together over Christmas. When she was finished, she paused to gather her thoughts.

"So let me get this straight: after only knowing this guy for a few weeks, you were ready to marry him and have his kids?" he asked skeptically.

Grace narrowed her eyes. "When you say it like that, it sounds stupid. And given the circumstances, it was stupid. But Christmas is the most magical time of the year. I must have gotten carried away by all that magic."

"There's nothing wrong with that," he said softly. "I didn't mean to make you feel stupid. I was just pointing out how little you actually know him."

"I know, and you're right. I don't know him nearly as well as I thought I did. We lived in the same house, though, celebrating the holidays together. I think that skewed reality a little."

Cole nodded at her explanation. "What happened next?"

"He left to go back home to New York. He was only supposed to be gone for a couple of weeks. Just long enough to pack up his apartment and tie up any loose ends. Instead, he was gone for a month. A few days after he left, he quit returning my calls and texts. When he finally arrived, he refused to talk to me. Said he needed time and asked me to be patient. Then, his girlfriend showed up, and now here we are." She took another drink, almost downing it in one gulp.

"You know, it's not even that he has a new girlfriend. It's the fact he lied. Why couldn't he just be a man and tell me the truth?" she asked, her words starting to slur.

Cole pushed the basket of wings toward her. "It sounds like he was hoping he could keep both of you on the hook until he made some kind of decision."

Grace shrugged. "That's a very jerk thing to do. Can I have another drink, please?"

Cole looked reluctant, but something in her expression convinced him to agree since he left to make her drink. When he returned, he held her glass just out of reach. "I will only give this to you when you've eaten at least half of your wings."

"Don't you have other customers to bother?" Grace grumbled as she rolled her eyes and picked up one of the wings. The effects of the alcohol had started to kick in, and for once, she felt good. Like, really good. Why was there always someone there trying to ruin that for her?

Cole laughed. "You're the only customer I care about. I can't have you passing out drunk in my bar. It's bad for business."

Grace rolled her eyes again. "I can't see how buying enough drinks to pass out could even remotely be considered bad for business. But whatever."

As the hours passed, Grace ate and drank while Cole entertained her with stories about other customers and experiences from his past. When he finally announced it was closing time, she looked around, surprised to discover she was the only one left in the bar. Where had everyone else gone? When had they gone? She honestly couldn't remember anything other than talking to Cole.

She tried to get off the bar stool and immediately lost her balance when the room spun. If Cole hadn't been there to catch her, she would have ended up face-first on the sticky floor. Holding on to him, she slowly made her way to the door. When they reached her car outside, she reached into her purse for her keys.

"I hope you realize you're in no shape to drive," he said, holding her upright.

She blinked at him, confused about what he expected her to do. There was no way she could walk home; she couldn't even make it to her car without help. "What do you expect me to do then?"

"I'll take you home. You can get your car tomorrow after you've sobered up."

"There's just one problem," Grace replied as she stared at the keys still in the ignition.

"What's that?"

Grace pointed to the keys. "I'm afraid I've locked myself out."

Cole stood silently for a minute, debating what to do. "I guess you'll have to come home with me," he sighed.

"You don't have to sound so excited about it," Grace slurred angrily. "I'll just walk home and sleep on the porch." She forcefully jerked her arm away from him and fell in the opposite direction. Once again, he caught her and brought her close to his chest, holding her in place with his strong arms.

"It's not that I don't want you there; I just don't want you there like this. You're drunk, and I don't want you to wake up in the morning and feel like I took advantage of you. Not that you'll have any reason to think that," he quickly added.

Grace nodded, unsure of what to say. She wasn't sure what he was talking about but figured he knew more than she did, so she would have to trust him. "I'm sorry," she said into his chest. Hot tears rolled down her cheeks. No matter how hard she tried, she kept making a mess of things.

"It's okay," he said, patting her back. "Let's just go home. We can figure everything else out in the morning."

She let him lead her to his truck and accepted his help getting in. Her fiery temper had been extinguished, exhaustion and embarrassment having taken its place. Resting her head against the cold window pane, she closed her eyes and let the noise from the road lull her to sleep. Maybe when she woke up, she would discover this had all been a dream. One could only hope.

-Days till Valentine's Day-

Ten

G race awoke with the worst headache she had ever had in her entire life. As she slowly opened her eyes, she looked around the dark and unfamiliar room, panic quickly setting in when she couldn't remember where she was or how she got there. Sitting up too fast for her aching head to handle, she felt the contents of last night's bad decisions lurch up her throat. Looking wildly around the room, she spotted the bucket someone had placed on the floor next to her. With great relief, she heaved into the bucket, praying she would feel better when she was done.

With a groan, she sat back on the couch, closed her eyes, and tried to figure out what to do. Seconds later, she heard a noise and opened her eyes to see Cole standing over her with a glass in one hand and what looked like a couple of aspirin in the other.

"Here," he said, handing both to her. "They'll help you feel better."

Grace reached out reluctantly and accepted the items, the room tilting slightly at the movement. "Thanks," she said with a wince. It took all her willpower to keep from vomiting again, but it was worth it. The last thing she wanted to do was throw up in front of him. She was pretty sure she would literally die from embarrassment.

Tossing the pills into her mouth, she washed them down with the horrid concoction he had handed her. "Oh my gosh, what is this?" she asked, certain he was trying to kill her.

"It's a cure for your hangover. I know it tastes nasty, but I promise you'll feel better once you've gotten it all down."

She gave him a sideways glance but did as she was told, too desperate to stop the world from spinning to argue. It took a while, but she eventually managed to empty the cup. "Thank you," she said, handing it back to him. "What happened last night?"

"Well, to make a long story short, you closed down the bar, locked your keys in your car, and passed out in the truck on the way here."

Grace nodded slowly, the events blurry but familiar, including the part where she cried in Cole's arms. Her cheeks reddened with embarrassment, which seemed to have become common with him. "I'm sorry," she finally said, covering her face with her hands.

"Hey," he said, sitting on the couch beside her and putting his arm around her shoulders. "It's okay."

"I may not be an expert at getting drunk, but I'm pretty certain it's not normal to end up on your bartender's couch. This is humiliating. I can't even begin to imagine what you must think of me right now."

"I think you are a beautiful, smart, kind, and capable woman who finally cracked under the stress and pressure you've been facing for the last five years. If ending up on my couch is the worst thing that happens, I'd say things are going pretty well."

Grace peeked at him from between her fingers. He looked sincere, but she didn't know him very well and couldn't be sure. "Do you mean that?"

"Of course I do. Wouldn't say it if I didn't."

"It's that simple with you huh?"

Cole shrugged and then sighed. "Life is too short for the games people like to play. I find it much easier to be honest and let the chips fall where they may. Not everyone will like it, but they'll never accuse me of lying."

Even in her current state, Grace could detect an undercurrent of pain in his words. She wanted to ask him about it but didn't feel like now was the time. "What time is it?" she asked instead.

Cole pulled his phone out of his pocket and turned on the screen. "It's almost ten," he replied.

"Oh my gosh," she exclaimed, her eyes wide as saucers. "It's so dark in here I was sure it was still early. I've missed breakfast, and oh my gosh, what is everyone going to think?"

"It's only dark because I closed the curtains so the sun wouldn't hurt your eyes. As for everyone else, I called Grant and told him where you are. I can assure you that his wife was not thrilled, but I was at least able to stop her from tearing apart the town looking for you."

"How do you know Grant?" she asked suspiciously.

"For goodness sake, Grace, haven't I proven I can be trusted by now?" When she opened her mouth to respond, he waved his hand in her direction dismissively. "Forget it. I met Grant a couple of weeks ago when he approached me about signing up for his new firm's financial services. We got to talking, and he told me about how he ended up here. So, it wasn't much of a stretch to figure out he'd be a good person to call about you."

"Thank you," she replied. She gave him an apologetic look. At some point, she would have to learn to stop sticking her foot in her mouth around this guy.

"I should get you back home." He got up, walked over to the kitchen counter, and picked up a set of keys. "Are you ready?"

Grace nodded and stood up slowly. She motioned to the bucket. "Is there somewhere I can clean this up?"

"Don't worry about it; I'll take care of it later."

He clearly wanted her out of his house, not that she blamed him. Ever since she showed up at the bar last night, she had been grumpy, insolent, sarcastic, and sometimes downright rude. He had deserved precisely none of the treatment he had received. There had to be a way she could make it up to him; she just couldn't seem to think of one.

Following him out of the house, she practically screamed when the bright sunlight hit her too-sensitive eyes.

"Here," he said, handing her a pair of sunglasses.

After putting them on, she instantly felt better. Physically anyway. Emotionally, she felt even worse. She was behaving like a brat, yet he still took care of her every step of the way. She would definitely have to find a way to make this up to him. The question was, how?

***

Since her keys were still locked in her car, Cole took her home so she could get the spare. He had planned to wait for her to retrieve the key and then take her down to the bar, but Molly came running out of the house as soon as they pulled up and waved him away. Grace tried to stop him so she could thank him again, but he had taken off before she could.

Already irritated with Molly, she snapped at her. "Why did you do that? He was only trying to help, and you just chased him off like he's some kind of criminal."

"In my book, he is a criminal for taking advantage of a young woman like that."

"Excuse me," Grace said. "Who did he take advantage of and how?"

"You, Grace. He took advantage of you. Are you really too naive to see that?"

"I have no idea what you're talking about, but you are out of line," Grace stomped toward the stairs, her head still hurting enough she had no interest in continuing this conversation, now or ever.

"You just spent the night with that guy," Molly hissed, yanking on Grace's arm to get her to stop. "Do you not see how inappropriate that is?"

"Not that it is any of your business, but I spent the night on his couch," she enunciated, "Because I locked my keys in my car, and he was kind enough not to leave me stranded in the middle of the street."

"Oh, well, explain how you ended up with him in the first place."

"Well, Mom, I ended up with him because I chose to go to his bar and ended up totally wasted. And since you're suddenly so interested in my life, let me enlighten you as to why I ended up wasted in his bar. That woman you invited to stay at my home, without even talking to me I might add, is Hunter's new girlfriend."

Molly gasped, her hand going to her mouth. "Are you serious? How do you know?"

"How do I know? Let me set the scene for you. I'm giving Rebekah a tour of my home when, all of a sudden, Hunter comes running in the door. Rebekah sees him, throws her arms around him, and starts going on about how much she missed her boyfriend. Right in front of me." Grace paused to catch her breath. "He couldn't even look me in the eye. He just stood there holding her while she went on and on about everything they're going to do together. Oh, and then I had to make them a romantic snack," Grace spit out.

The look on Molly's face was priceless. If Grace wasn't so angry, she might have laughed.

"I'm so sorry, I had no idea," Molly said as she shook her head in disbelief.

Grace shrugged as the anger seeped from her body, leaving her numb. It had been a whirlwind twenty-four hours, and now, she only wanted to crawl into bed and pretend the rest of the world no longer existed. Unfortunately, she couldn't do that; she still had an inn to run, whether she wanted to or not. "Since you scared off my ride, can you at least take me to get my car?"

"Of course, just let me run home and get my keys."

"Sounds good; I still need to get my spare. I'll meet you back here in a couple of minutes." Grace said as she headed for the front door. Once inside, she checked on Granny and Gladys, thankful they were doing well and none the wiser about her late-night activities.

After grabbing her key, she returned downstairs, carefully avoiding Hunter and Rebekah. She wouldn't be able to avoid them forever, but she was for darn sure going to try to avoid them as much as possible. Which would be easier to do once the other guests arrived. Unfortunately, to her knowledge, no additional guests had even signed up. And even if they had, there was still an entire week to get through before they arrived. It was going to be a long week.

-Days till Valentine's Day-

Nine

Sunday morning, Grace found herself back in the kitchen making breakfast. Surprisingly, she had slept well the night before for the first time in almost a month. It was almost as if her night at the bar had exorcised the demons that had kept her from resting. In fact, she felt so good she almost didn't mind when Rebekah and Hunter came downstairs for breakfast hand-in-hand. Almost.

If she were honest, the sight of them together still stung, but the sting had lessened significantly. Now, instead of the pain of being dumped, it was the lack of closure that bothered her most. The feeling that she wasn't significant enough in his life to warrant an explanation and an official parting of ways gnawed on her emotions. For someone who already suffered from low self-esteem and feelings of unworthiness, this hit where she felt weakest.

Despite her feelings, she did her best to provide a breakfast worthy of a five-star restaurant. Whether she succeeded or not was up for debate. After they finished eating, Grace cleaned the kitchen, her mind occupied by thoughts of someone other than Hunter. She owed Cole big-time and wanted to do something special to make up for how she'd treated him. Not only had he proved to be a great friend, he was also a business partner she could not afford to lose.

When Hunter appeared mid-way through her cleaning, she was more than a little annoyed. "Is there something I can do for you?" she asked in as professional a voice as she could muster.

"Are you trying to make me jealous?" he asked, a hint of anger in his otherwise laid-back and mellow voice.

"Excuse me? Is this some kind of sick joke?"

"You stayed out all night the other night. From what I overheard; you were with some man. That is not normal behavior for you, so I will ask again: are you trying to make me jealous?"

"You have a lot of nerve asking me a question like that when your girlfriend is upstairs," she said, enunciating the word girlfriend. "What I do and who I do it with is none of your business."

"Look, I'm sorry about Rebekah, I should have told you about her, but I had no idea she would show up like this."

"Yes, you should have told me about her, not because she showed up, but because it was the decent thing to do." Grace took a breath to calm her anger. "I asked you repeatedly to tell me what was going on with you. You had numerous chances to tell me the truth, so why didn't you?"

Hunter was quiet for so long Grace was sure he would refuse to answer. When he finally opened his mouth to speak, she did her best to remain silent and listen.

"Rebekah and I have known each other pretty much our entire lives. Our families have been friends for decades and often joked about us growing up and getting married. At some point, it stopped being a joke." He paused as he ran his hand through his hair. "We were in love but wanted different things out of life. I was a career-minded kind of guy while she wanted to travel the world. We did our best to make it work, but at some point, it became clear we were just too different, so we split up. She was always the one that got away."

He pulled out a chair and sat down. "If you remember, back in December, I realized I wasn't happy with my career anymore. I was burned out and felt like I was missing out on the important things in life." He reached out and took her hand. "At the time, I really did believe I could be happy here with you." He looked up into her eyes, his sadness mirrored in her own.

"So what happened?"

"When I got back to New York, I ran into Rebekah. She had come home to visit her family for the holidays, and we just...reconnected I guess. It was like old times again, yet everything was new, too. I didn't plan to get back together with her; it just sort of happened. The next thing I knew, she asked me to travel with her. Last time she did that, I refused," he said with a shrug. "But this time was different. This time, it sounded exciting. It felt like I was being given a chance to catch up on everything I had missed out on when I chose to put my career ahead of everything else."

"Why didn't you just tell me? I would have understood. Would have tried to anyway."

"Because every time I thought about you, I had doubts. I enjoyed my time here with you, Grace, and I could still see settling down here and having a life. So, I decided to come back and see how I felt. I didn't want to tell you the truth in case I decided to stay here instead."

Grace's eyes went wide at his explanation. "You planned to completely alienate me, come back here to see whether or not you wanted to stay, and then what? If you decided to stay, you expected me to just run back into your open arms, no explanations necessary?"

He crinkled his nose in disdain. "It sounds kind of crappy when you say it like that."

"Because it is crappy. The way you treated me was horrible. Whether you intended to or not, you did a lot of damage to our relationship. To me, personally. I've spent countless sleepless nights wondering what I did wrong."

He reached across the counter and took her hand in his again. "I'm so sorry. You didn't do anything wrong. I—"

"Hunter? Are you down here?" Rebekah called out as she came around the corner. "Oh, there you are." She came up behind him and wrapped her arms around his neck as Hunter quickly snatched his hand back from Grace's. "What are you two talking about?" she asked innocently.

When Hunter remained quiet, Grace spoke up. "We were discussing dinner. Is there anything, in particular, you would like?"

"Hunter and I had plans to go out for a romantic night on the town," she said, squeezing his arms. "I don't suppose you know a place you could recommend?"

"The only place I know of is called Bella's. It's an Italian restaurant up in the city."

Hunter winced at the mention of the restaurant he had taken her to not that long ago. He shot her a pained glance and then stood up, excusing himself from the room. Both Grace and Rebekah watched him go.

When he was out of earshot, Rebekah turned to Grace. "I can see why he likes this place," she said, looking around the room. "It's quaint, the perfect place for a vacation."

Grace nodded, unsure of where she was going with this. Luckily, she didn't have to wait long to find out. "What it's not is the kind of place a man like Hunter settles down in. He is far too sophisticated and worldly to fit into a backwoods place like this. No offense," she added quickly.

"None taken. I wouldn't exactly consider us 'backwoods,' but our small-town way of life isn't for everyone."

"Let's just cut to the chase, shall we? Hunter and I are soulmates. We've been destined to be together since we were born. Whatever illusions you have of him picking you and staying here forever, it's time to get rid of them."

Grace nodded. "Understood."

"I'm serious," she said, putting her finger in Grace's face. "I have never lost a competition; I'm not about to start now."

Grace pushed her finger out of her face, her patience wearing thin. "I have zero desire to compete with you for anyone's affection, including Hunter's. As far as I'm concerned, he's yours. So whatever illusions you have about some big competition between us, it's time for you to get rid of them. Now, if you'll excuse me, I have work to do."

Rebekah watched her for a moment, her eyes narrowed and calculating. "I'm glad we've come to an understanding. I'm sure I don't have to remind you how detrimental one negative comment from me would be to your business."

"No, you don't have to remind me. Obviously, I can't stop you from doing what you wish, but I do hope you will consider the implications your actions will have on me and my family before you make such a decision. Once you and Hunter leave, and make no mistake, I fully expect the two of you to leave together; we still have to live our lives. Not all of us were born into privilege..." she trailed off, hoping Rebekah got her meaning.

"Stay out of my way, and not only will I not post something negative, I'll do you a solid and give you a rave review," she stuck out her hand. "Deal?"

Grace shook her hand. "Deal."

"Good, it was nice talking to you, Grace."

"Likewise," she responded.

Rebekah turned on her heel and left, leaving Grace to mull over the conversation they had just had. Her only choice had been to accept Rebekah's offer, anything less would have been career suicide. Yet, she felt like she had made a deal with the devil. It was an icky feeling, but what else could she do?

Determined to move on and put everything that had just happened behind her, she opened up her giant recipe book and began to search through the dessert section. It was the one area she had neglected to practice, and now that she had some free time, it seemed as good a time as any to start. Then, an idea hit her. What if she invited Cole to dinner? A man who lived alone and spent most nights eating bar food would appreciate a home-cooked meal.

Pulling out her phone, she sent him a text inviting him to dinner that night. When the little response dots immediately flashed on her screen, she breathed a sigh of relief. At least he wasn't so angry he would ignore her. A few seconds later, his response popped up, 'Love to, what time?'. She typed in six o'clock and hit send. A second later, the thumbs-up emoji flashed on her screen.

Smiling to herself, she pulled on her apron and got to work. Six o'clock would likely come fast, and she wanted to be ready.

-Days till Valentine's Day-

Eight

Grace was attempting to make custard tarts in the kitchen when Molly walked in, laptop in hand.

"Do you mind if I work here for a while?" she asked.

"Not at all," Grace replied. "I could use a taste tester. Out of curiosity, what's wrong with your office?"

"Ugh," Molly groaned. "Rebekah decided to accompany Hunter to work this morning. After listening to her incessant baby talk for over an hour, I just couldn't take it anymore."

Grace nodded but chose to say nothing, instead focusing on the crust she was shaping. In her opinion, Rebekah was highly annoying, but she was pretty sure her opinion was more than a little biased. Unable to resist the urge any longer, she cracked. "She couldn't have been any more insufferable than she was at breakfast," Grace said, raising her brow.

Molly laughed. "Yeah, that was pretty bad too. It was almost as if she knew about you and Hunter and was trying to twist the knife, what with all that talk of their romantic date last night." Molly watched Grace make a face. "Oh, she does know about you and Hunter."

"Yep, she confronted me about him yesterday after breakfast."

"So we can add cruel to her list of annoying character traits. Honestly, I don't know what he sees in her. As far as I'm concerned, there's no contest between the two of you."

"Thanks," Grace gave her a small smile. "Hunter told me they grew up together, so he probably sees her a little differently than we do."

Molly tilted her head as she thought about that, then shrugged. "I suppose. How are you holding up? It couldn't have been easy to hear her talk about that."

"I'm fine," Grace said as she moved on to the next tart. When Molly continued to stare at her, she stopped and sighed. "I was really hurt when Hunter began treating me differently, and it really hurt that he chose to lie instead of being honest with me. But, a part of me had already accepted this outcome. I have zero desire to be with a man who can easily disregard me and my feelings, you know?"

"That makes sense. You deserve to be treated better than he's been treating you. From what I've heard, there's a new man in your life. Could that be the reason you're handling things so well? Have you already moved on?"

"If you're referring to Cole, he and I are just friends."

"A little birdie told me the two of you had a date of your own last night."

"If you consider playing cards with Granny and Gladys a date, then yes, I guess we did," Grace laughed.

"That might not be considered the epitome of romance, but you have to admit, you've been spending a lot of time together lately."

"I've only seen him four times in the last week, and half of those involved work," Grace protested. She wasn't sure what it was, but something about this conversation made her nervous. Dinner last night was a lot of fun. The food had turned out to be edible, which had been a considerable relief, and Grace had finally managed to make it through an encounter with Cole that didn't involve sticking her foot in her mouth or embarrassing herself somehow.

"It's probably too soon to be talking about another romance," Molly said quietly, a look of chagrin on her face.

Grace put her tart tins on a large baking sheet and popped them in the oven before walking around the counter and sitting at the table opposite Molly. "I appreciate your concern, but everything is fine. I've accepted that Hunter has moved on, and I'm enjoying forming a friendship with Cole. He's one of our new partners, and I feel it's important to be on good terms with the people we're doing business with. Anything beyond that..." Grace trailed off, unsure of what to say. Her feelings for Cole were too new and somewhat complicated to dissect. "Anyway, have we had any bites on the marketing campaign?" Grace asked, effectively changing the subject and ending the discussion about her love life.

Molly opened up her laptop and powered it on. "Let's see, I was too distracted this morning and forgot to check my emails," she said apologetically.

Grace waited while she scrolled through the hundreds of emails that had come in over the weekend. Last time, Grace had been the one to get the emails from prospective guests. This time, Molly had decided to handle it to make the division of labor between them more equitable. From the looks of things, it would have been better if Grace had remained in charge.

"Okay," she finally said. "Looks like we have a couple of emails. One is from Vanessa," she said as she scanned the email. "Vanessa says she is the only single in her friend group and is tired of being left out around the holidays. She says she would love the opportunity to focus on herself and spend a few stress-free days with other like-minded people."

Grace nodded. "She sounds like a perfect fit. Who's the other one from?"

Molly clicked her mouse a couple of times and scanned some more. "This one's from a man named Emilio. He has a job interview on the Monday before Valentine's Day and would love to come and meet some people to get a feel for the area. The planned events sound fun and a good way to keep his stress levels down before the big interview."

Grace scrunched her nose. "Not exactly what I was going for, but it sounds like he's willing to participate, so..." Grace thought about it for a minute. "Does he mention the company he's interviewing with? If it's somewhere up in the city, which it likely is, he may not realize how far away we are from where he ultimately wants to end up."

"Actually, I think he might be the guy Grant is planning to interview." Molly got out her phone and texted Grant. A few minutes later, her phone dinged, and she checked his response. "Yep, it's the same guy. Do you think that'll be weird? Or some kind of conflict of interest or something?"

"I have no idea. You should talk to Grant about that and, depending on what he says, disclose the information to Emilio. He might decide hanging out with his potential boss before the interview isn't quite the stress-free weekend he thought it would be."

"I'll talk to Grant and let you know. I'll also accept Vanessa's booking and send her the payment information. Hopefully, a few more options will trickle in over the next few days."

"Hopefully. Last time, we filled up so fast I barely had time to stress over it. This time, things are taking a bit longer, which is scary. I thought we had a slam-dunk with this one."

"Oh, we definitely have a home run on our hands. I forgot to tell you, we've sold over five hundred tickets to the murder mystery!"

Grace's eyes went wide. "Five hundred? That's insane. How on earth are we going to handle that many people?"

"It's not as many as you think. We served that many people pancakes in like three hours at Christmas. And that was in one building. Remember, this event will be spread around town, so we could easily accommodate up to a thousand."

"That's a lot of food to prepare. I better check with Bea and Addie to see if they need help. Since I will be hosting the actual crime scene here in the house, we could set up a serving station in the dining room, and I could make the food for our location."

"Wow, I'm impressed!" Molly smiled.

Grace blushed. "I'm sure my food will pale in comparison, but I'm willing to help lighten their load if they need me to."

"I'm sure they'll appreciate it, just don't wear yourself out. They're used to cooking for large crowds. You've already taken on more than you're used to by cooking for the inn that weekend."

"I'm sure I'll be fine. I can sleep when I die, right?" Grace tried to laugh, but it came out as a strangled gurgle. The truth was, she was terrified. Her cooking had drastically improved, but it was still unlikely to win any awards. Hopefully, people will have such a good time they won't notice her portion of food is lacking.

"Oh, looks like another email just came in," Molly exclaimed excitedly. "This one is from a woman named Jane. She says she hates how commercialized all the holidays have become and is looking forward to spending time in a place that is 'anti-Valentine's Day,'" Molly said, using air quotes. She looked up at Grace and made a face. "I'm not sure she's going to be a lot of fun..."

"Maybe, I don't know. None of our events are catering to Valentine's Day, nor do they mention it; she might be perfectly fine," Grace said, though she sounded as unsure as she felt. The goal was not to be 'anti-Valentine's Day' but to offer a fun alternative for people who were usually expected to sit this one out.

"Let's keep her on the maybe list for another day or two. If no one else shows any interest, we'll accept her."

"Sounds good." The oven dinged, so Grace got up to check her tart crusts. When they came out looking exactly like they were supposed to, she excitedly pumped her fist in the air. If she keeps this up, she might end up in the running for those awards after all.

Molly closed her laptop and gathered her things. "I'm going to talk to Grant. Wish me luck," she said, rolling her eyes.

"Good luck," Grace called out cheerfully, glad it was Molly and not her who had to deal with the two lovebirds.

Once she had finished filling her tarts with custard, she put them back in the oven to bake and then made a three-way call to Bea and Addie. "Hey ladies, I just heard the news about all the tickets we've sold to the murder mystery dinner."

"Isn't it wonderful!" Bea said excitedly. "Over five hundred, and we still have almost a week to go. Who knows, we might just reach a thousand!"

"Ugh," Addie groaned. "As awesome as that would be, I already feel like I'm drowning over here. That is way too much food for me to handle."

"That's actually why I'm calling," Grace interjected. "As you both know, I'm hosting one of the locations at the house. Would it help if we set up a serving station here and I made the food for it?"

"Are you sure you're up for that?" Bea asked hesitantly. "You're already in charge of all the food for your guests."

"I can handle it. I plan to make a bunch of appetizer-style foods. That will be a lot easier than trying to make meal-sized food.

"I will gladly accept your offer," said Addie. "Thank you, Grace, this will help a lot."

"I'll accept it too," Bea relented. "But if you need help, promise to let me know."

"I promise, and if you'd like to take a break in a little while and sample some of my newest creations, you are more than welcome to come by. Both of you. It might put your mind at ease to see the improvement I've made.

"That sounds like fun; Lord knows, I could use a break!" replied Addie.

"Sounds good to me, too," said Bea. "How about we stop by in about an hour?"

"Works for me. See you then," Grace replied. She clicked the end-call button and got back to work. She would be in business if she could convince Bea and Addie that her cooking had improved. Why this meant so much to her, she had no idea. Something else she needed to think about and reflect on.

-Days till Valentine's Day-

Seven

Tempted by the nicer-than-usual weather, Grace chose to walk down to town hall for the meeting with Mayor Allen. It would be awesome if the temperature would hold through the weekend since a large part of the murder mystery dinner would take place outside. Unfortunately, a cold front was predicted to move in over the next few days, with flurries expected Friday night. She really hoped the weather wouldn't impact the event they had worked so hard to put on.

When she finally arrived, she saw she was the last one there; everyone else already seated and talking amongst themselves.

"There you are," Mayor Allen called out when he saw her enter the room. "Attention, everyone, it's time to call this meeting to order."

Grace felt a blush creep up her cheeks at the realization they had been waiting for her to start the meeting. She sat between Molly and Bea and tried her best to blend into the background.

"Grace," said Mayor Allen. "I trust you took care of that little problem we discussed last week?"

So much for blending into the background. "Yes, Sir," she replied. "We're going to partner with Cole and his bar."

Mayor Allen nodded. "That's a great idea. Not only does it solve our problem, it gets another business owner involved with the community. What about the food stations? We need to make sure those are up to code as well. Don't want any problems with the health department."

"The food stations will be located inside establishments already licensed to sell food. We're writing the mystery to include those locations so it makes sense and stays in keeping with the theme." Grace answered, somewhat nervous to again have all the attention on her. You would think by now she would have gotten used to it. You would be wrong. She wasn't sure there would ever come a day when she was comfortable speaking in front of a crowd. Even a small crowd full of people she'd known for most of her life.

Mayor Allen nodded again as he took notes in the notebook on his desk. "Sounds good; where are we at with the ticket sales?"

Finally, a question she was not expected to answer, Grace thought, sighing a little in relief. She listened as Molly gave her answer.

"At last count, we are now up to six hundred and thirty-five tickets sold."

Mayor Allen gave a low whistle. "That is a much larger number than I think any of us anticipated. Good job, ladies," he said, smiling approvingly at Molly and Grace. "Are we confident we can make enough food to feed everyone?"

"We're fairly confident," Addie answered. "I may have to close the diner on Saturday to get everything done, but if the number keeps increasing, it should be worth it."

"I agree," Bea chimed in. "Between the three of us and our staff, we should be able to handle it."

"Three of you?" Mayor Allen asked.

"Addie, Grace, and I," Bea answered.

Mayor Allen turned his attention back to Grace. "You're going to provide food for the dinner?" he asked, his brows raised.

Jeez, she thought, did everyone in town know about her terrible cooking skills?

"She's turning into quite the chef," Bea interjected, sparing Grace the embarrassment of having to defend herself. "Addie and I went to the inn yesterday for a taste test and were very impressed."

Addie nodded her head in agreement. "If she didn't already have a job, I'd hire her myself."

Grace's cheeks turned fire engine red. She ducked her head in hopes no one would see. After a moment, she felt Bea pat her back and started feeling better.

Mayor Allen cleared his throat. "Okay then, does anyone else have anything to discuss?" He looked around the room, then dismissed the meeting when no one said anything or raised their hand. "I would like everyone to meet her again Friday morning to review any last-minute details.

In the meantime, please don't hesitate to reach out if you have any questions or concerns."

With that, he stood up and left the room. Grace immediately jumped up and followed him out, too embarrassed to talk to anyone and risk being teased. When she made it safely outside, she checked her watch to see it was only two thirty. Cole's bar wouldn't open for another two and a half hours. She could text him to see if he could meet now but ultimately decided against it. She didn't want to make a nuisance of herself. That decision made, she headed home to do more cooking. They say practice makes perfect; she could only hope 'they' were right.

***

Five o'clock came and went, then six o'clock, then seven o'clock. It was now eight, and Grace was desperate to leave the house. The plan had been to have dinner on the table at six, cleaned up by seven, and out of the house by seven fifteen at the latest. But no, here she was, still at home, forced to cater to the ridiculous demands of her guest.

Rebekah had decided she was in the mood for some exotic, hard-to-pronounce dessert she had experienced during one of her recent European trips. Grace, usually happy to accommodate, had tried her best, but acquiring half the ingredients typically used in the recipe was impossible. What she had ultimately ended up with was the dessert's poor country cousin, and Rebekah was just not having it.

In an attempt to appease her, Grace had tried option number two, an equally tricky dessert, and was thus still stuck at home waiting on the oven. If Rebekah had been her first guest, she would have closed the bed-and-breakfast for good, money be darned. When the timer went off, she assembled the dessert to look as social media-worthy as possible, dropped it off outside her door, and then dashed out of there before Rebekah could complain again.

It was eight thirty when she finally arrived at Cole's bar. She went inside, slid onto the same bar stool she had used the other night, and waited to get his attention. It was far less crowded this time, with only half as many people as before. When he finally saw her, he smiled, and she breathed a sigh of relief. It was so nice to see a friendly face after the night she'd had.

"Back for round two?" he grinned.

"I could probably use a drink, but I'm here to talk to you about the mystery dinner. We finally got everything worked out," she smiled back at him, his grin infectious.

"How about I get you a coke, and then you can give me all the details?"

Grace nodded in agreement; a coke seemed like the next best thing. He returned a moment later, drink in hand, and she gratefully took a sip, the day's stress melting away. "It's a good thing this is just a coke; otherwise, I'd be a little concerned."

"Why's that?"

"Because this place seems to make me feel better. I'd hate to discover I have some sort of alcohol dependency," she said as she crinkled her nose.

Cole laughed. "I bet it's the company that makes you feel better, not the alcohol," he teased.

"You're probably right," Grace answered with a serious expression.

"Things still pretty rough at home?"

"Yes, but not in the way you might be thinking. My new guest has become...demanding. It's already a stressful time, what with the events we're planning; her demands add a new level of stress and pressure I didn't sign up for."

"I guess that's part and parcel in the hospitality business."

Grace made a face at him. "Maybe so, but that doesn't mean I have to like it."

"You didn't run into any problems like this with your last batch of guests?"

"No," she said, shaking her head for emphasis. "My last group of guests was pretty awesome. I imagine that's part of the problem. She's standing out in all the wrong ways."

"I feel for you," he said sympathetically.

"I'm sure you get your fair share of difficult customers...," she said, looking down at the bar.

"You are not a difficult customer, silly," he replied. "I had a great time with you the other night. Snarky attitude and all."

"You are way nicer to me than I deserve," she said, looking into his eyes.

He leaned his forearms on the bar so he was eye-level with her. Reaching forward, he clasped one of her hands between his and began to play with one of the rings on her fingers. "What I think you deserve and what you think you deserve seem to be very different things."

Grace wanted to respond but didn't know what to say, so she watched him instead. When the tension became too much to bear, she awkwardly cleared her throat. "I guess I should give you those details," she stammered.

He smiled at her, clearly aware of his effect on her. Seeming to take pity on her, he released her hand and stood up straight. "What do you have for me?"

"Um, we're going to have three serving stations. One at Bea's Bakery, one at Addie's Diner, and one at my house. So, if possible, we'll need you to set up at each location."

"That sounds doable. I found a couple of carts in the back I think Ted used to set up at fairs and other similar events. We should be able to use those. I hope disposable cups will be acceptable. I'm not interested in hunting down my bar glasses all over town."

Grace smiled at the image. "We could always turn it into a scavenger hunt. The person who finds the most glasses wins a prize!"

Cole seemed to consider that. "Could be fun, but if it's all the same, these glasses aren't cheap."

Grace laughed. "I was teasing you; of course, disposable cups are fine. I know a supplier where we can get plastic versions of wine and beer glasses. I've been told we should prepare to host around a thousand people. So if you can give me an idea of how many glasses you'll need, I'll try to track them down."

"It's kind of late for that, isn't it? I mean, the dinner is in four days."

"I might make a few cross-country trips, but it will be worth it. Plus, I can leave Molly in charge of the inn. It's her turn to deal with the guest from you know where."

"Tell you what, find out where we need to get the supplies, and I'll go with you. There's no way you'll fit everything we need in your little car. My truck has much more room, and I have a small trailer if we need it."

Grace had a flashback to an earlier conversation between her and Hunter. It had gone much the same as this one, and the similarities made her very uncomfortable. Was she making the same mistake twice?

"Hey," he said, lifting her chin with his finger to meet his gaze. "What just happened? All of a sudden, you just went...melancholy or something. Did I say something wrong?"

Grace shook her head and tried to smile, it not quite reaching her eyes. "It's nothing, just trying to figure out logistics in my mind," she lied.

He didn't look like he believed her, but let it go anyway.

"How much do I owe you for the coke?" she asked as she pulled a couple of bills out of her purse.

"It's on the house," he said, waving her money away. "You don't have to go," he said softly.

She took a deep breath and let it out slowly. Going home held zero appeal, but staying felt dangerous. The more time she spent with Cole, the more she wanted to spend with him. He was another man way out of her league, and if her experience with Hunter had taught her anything, relationships like that rarely lasted very long.

No, she was much better off risking another dessert disaster at home than risking her heart by staying here with Cole. "I need to go track down those locations," she explained. "As you pointed out, there are only four more days, and I need at least two to prepare for the event."

Cole nodded, disappointment on his face. "Let me know when you're ready to go."

"I will; thanks for the coke," she said, smiling at him. She turned and left before he could say anything else, her resolve to go lessening with each look he gave her. She needed to stay strong. At some point, Hunter would leave, taking all the tension and awkwardness with him. Cole was here for good, which meant the risk to her heart was even greater. A fact she would do well to remember.

-Days till Valentine's Day-

Six

When Grace woke up, she checked her phone and saw she had a message from Cole. The time stamp showed he had sent it around six that morning, which made her feel extremely lazy since it was now eight, and she knew the bar didn't close until eleven on weeknights. The guy likely ran around on six hours of sleep, which seemed unfathomable.

Since it was time to make breakfast, she decided to put off responding until after everyone had eaten and, hopefully, left for the day. She barely reached the door to her room when her phone rang. Seeing it was Cole, she briefly debated ignoring it but then decided she was being childish and unfair. "Hello," she answered, somewhat nervously.

"Good morning. I hope I didn't wake you?" he drawled, his accent more pronounced over the phone.

"I just got up, unlike you, it would seem. How on earth do you function on so little sleep?"

He laughed. "Lots and lots of coffee." There was a pause in the conversation, both of them waiting for the other to speak. Finally, Cole broke the silence. "Did you get my message?"

"Yes," she responded, guilt rushing over her. "I was going to respond after breakfast."

"Okay, no worries. I'm planning my day here, and I need to know what the schedule looks like for you. I've got a lot of animals out here I need to make sure will be taken care of if you don't think we'll be back in time."

This was it, her chance to get out of going with him. "Honestly, Cole, I can take care of this by myself. You're a busy man, and I don't want to take up any more of your time than I already have," she winced, knowing she sounded lame but unable to do anything about it.

He sucked in his breath. "I'll be there at nine. Be ready to go and have your list. I'll line someone up for the evening feed, but if we need to be gone longer than that, I expect you to let me know by the time I get there."

Grace opened her mouth to respond when she heard a click. A glance at her phone showed he had ended the call. Well, she thought to herself, that took a lot of nerve. What is with men thinking they can always tell everyone what to do? Even though she couldn't fit the supplies in her car, and it was also his reputation on the line, did he really have the right to insert himself into her problems?

Seeing as how she had answered her own question, she decided to just go with it. She was the one with the nerve.

Here he was, going out of his way to help her with her event, and instead of being grateful, she was once again being a jerk, all because she couldn't keep her emotions under control. Something that was one hundred percent not his fault.

She hurried through breakfast, placed Molly in charge of Granny and Gladys for the day, and then grabbed her things, walking out the door as he pulled up to the curb. After climbing up into the cab of his truck, she put her seatbelt on and handed him the list of stores. Ten of them were located within an hour's drive. They could get every-thing they needed at the first ten if they were lucky. The second ten were located at least two hours away, and it only got worse from there. It could quickly turn into a very long day.

After studying the list, Cole put the truck in gear and pulled away from the curb. "Okay, out with it," he said, eyes on the road.

"What do you mean? Out with what?"

"Please don't play dumb with me. We both know some-thing happened last night at the bar. I can handle whatever it is you have to tell me. I can't handle you refusing to tell me the truth."

Grace swallowed the lump in her throat, embarrassed at being called out like this. Did she have the courage to tell him the truth? Did she have a choice? She was the one who just recently called Hunter out for not being honest; now that she was in the same boat, she had a deeper appreciation for how difficult it was to open up and allow yourself to be vulnerable with someone.

Clearing her throat, she took the plunge. "When you offered to go with me to pick up supplies, it reminded me of when I first met Hunter. One of the first things we did together was go up to the city, in his truck, to buy supplies for the bed-and-breakfast."

"So I brought up bad memories or something? I'm not sure I understand."

"Not exactly," she said with a sigh. "I felt like I was experiencing a case of deja vu. It reminded me of how stupid I was for flirting with you."

"Okkaayyy," he drawled. "I'm still not following."

"Look," Grace said, frustration clear in her voice. "You are a very nice, funny, kind, and incredibly handsome man. Most women would give their right arm for a chance to date you, me included. But, just like Hunter, you are clearly out of my league. So my flirting with you and trying to be 'friends' or whatever is very foolish. More so, when you consider we're currently partnering together for the events we have coming up."

Grace took a deep breath and then sighed. Telling him the truth had not set her free; it only deepened her embarrassment. She wished she could have put this conversation off until the end of the trip. It would indeed be a long day, regardless of how much time they spent on the road.

A few minutes later, Cole turned his blinker on and then turned onto a side road. Cringing a little at the thought her admission had caused him to change his mind about shopping with her, she prepared for him to turn around and take them back home. He surprised her by pulling off to the side of the road instead. Once the truck was in park, he left it running but took his seat belt off and turned to face her.

"It is very flattering you think so highly of me," he said slowly. "What I don't like is how low you see yourself."

She surprised herself by automatically turning in her seat to face him. "That's not what I'm doing, okay? The facts are the facts, regardless of how we feel about them. And the fact is, you're out of my league. I tried to pretend that didn't matter with Hunter, but I was clearly wrong. Men like you guys," she shook her head. "Men like you prefer the kind of woman I'm never going to be."

"And what kind of woman is that?"

"I don't know, a woman like Rebekah. Or Molly. A woman who's sophisticated and worldly. I've spent my entire adult life living like a hermit. I have nothing to show for my life." Tears stung her eyes, and she looked down at her lap in an attempt to hide them.

"Honey," he said, lifting her chin. "I appreciate that you didn't turn into a man-hater just because one of us did you wrong. But going in the opposite direction and believing you aren't worthy of love just because one man was stupid enough to let you go is also not okay. Besides, don't you think I should get a say in the kind of woman I want?"

She looked up at him through the top of her lashes. "I guess. But that doesn't mean you want me."

Cole sighed. "I'm really enjoying getting to know you. I've had a lot of fun with you and would like to see where things go. But I think we need to take things slow. A lot is going on in here," he said, pointing to her head. "A lot I think you need to work through."

Grace nodded. "I've already been thinking that. I feel like I might have a lot of unresolved fears and feelings surrounding my parent's death. My thoughts sometimes become irrational. The thing with Hunter didn't help."

"When did your parents die?"

"When I was five."

He sucked in a breath. "My gosh, Grace, I'm so sorry."

She gave a small smile. "Thanks. It's been a long time. I'm mostly over it. It's the lingering fears of abandonment that still get to me."

Cole pulled her onto his lap and wrapped his arms around her. "One thing I can promise is that I'm not going anywhere. Even if we never move beyond the friend phase, you'll always be able to count on me."

She wrapped her arms around his neck and rested her head against his chest. "Thank you. I'm not sure I deserve your promise, but I appreciate it."

He gave her one last hug and then let go, helping her back to her side of the truck. "Now that we've got that settled, how about we tackle this list of yours?"

"Sounds good to me," she said, relief washing over her. Maybe the truth does set people free. She certainly felt better now that she got all that off her chest.

"What are the chances we can get everything we need up here in the city?"

"If the websites are correct, the chances are high. If not..." she trailed off. Hopefully, the in-stock counts were correct, but you never knew until you got there. Cole had estimated they needed at least five thousand cups to be safe. Any leftovers could be used at the Valentine's Day event. She feared they would run out of glasses and have to make a second trip but would cross that bridge when she got to it. While she strongly believed in being prepared, she could only handle one event of this size at a time. Any more, and she might end up committed to the nearest institution.

The rest of the day with Cole was fun and somewhat magical, at least for her. They talked and laughed and told stories from their childhoods. It took a trip to all ten stores, but they managed to fill their order and were thus spared a trip to the next city, two hours away. She was happy and sad about that at the same time. Happy they had been able to get what they needed, sad the trip was now over.

They got back to town just in time for Grace to make dinner. Another thing she was less than thankful for. When dinner was finished, it took all her strength not to run down to the bar. Life always seemed a little brighter when she was with him, and she didn't relish a night home alone, especially one that would be spent with the obnoxious woman two doors down. But she managed to refrain, her desire to not seem clingy winning out. It was a shame because Rebekah's list of demands for the night rivaled the ones from the night before. Oh well, at least she was getting plenty of much-needed practice. Her guests would end up with five-star quality food at the rate she was going. She didn't know anyone who would complain about that, including Rebekah.

-Days till Valentine's Day-

Five

Another day, another breakfast Grace had to force herself to smile through while listening to Rebekah drone on and on about her 'amazing' relationship with Hunter. It was clear she was only doing it for Grace's benefit, and Grace wished there was a way to make her stop. This was the behavior her guests were coming to avoid, and they would be very unhappy if she continued once they arrived.

In a way, she felt sorry for the woman. The fact she felt the need to stake her claim every single time Grace was around made her look insecure and somewhat desperate. That was a position Grace hoped to never find herself in. In fact, it was one of the reasons it had been so easy to let him go. She couldn't fathom being in a relationship with someone whose affections she had to fight so hard for.

"So Grace," Molly said, interrupting one of Rebekah's long-winded stories. "Were you able to get everything you needed yesterday?"

"Thankfully, yes," she replied. "We had to go to all ten stores to do it, but we managed to find all five thousand cups. I also found the cutest detective-themed plates and napkins. I can't wait to show them to you; I'm pretty sure they'll be a hit."

"Sounds good. Is there anything else you need before Saturday?"

"I need to make another run to the store, but other than that, I think we're good." She turned to address Rebekah and Hunter. "If you two are interested, I have tickets for both of you. Also, we'll be hosting one of the locations. The upstairs will be off-limits, but there will be a lot of activity here that night."

"I don't know," Rebekah crinkled her nose in distaste. "It sounds kind of hokey."

"Well, you still have a couple of days to decide." Grace had to try really hard to keep from rolling her eyes. The nerve of this woman. Hoping to end her nightmare, Grace stood up and started stacking plates. A couple of them got the hint and stood to leave, but to her chagrin, the main offenders remained seated.

"I heard you went up to the city yesterday in a big ol' truck," Hunter stated, his eyebrow raised.

"Yes, that's correct. Why?" she asked, returning his stare.

"Just seems a little hypocritical, that's all."

"I'm not sure I follow; in what way is my going to the city to pick up supplies in a truck hypocritical?"

"Don't you remember the discussion we had about my truck? You claimed it was impractical and a waste of money. Seems like you've changed your mind," he said, an accusatory look on his face.

"What I said," Grace replied somewhat sternly, "Is that using a truck as a daily driver between here and the city would be costly in gas mileage and wear and tear on the vehicle. I never said I hated trucks."

"Guess your opinion must have changed when you started 'hanging out' with the new guy," he said, making air quotes with his fingers.

Grace rolled her eyes. "Cole is hardly a new guy; he's lived here his whole life. And not that it's any of your business, but we took his truck because we needed it to haul supplies back home from the city. Which is as practical as you're going to get." She picked up the stack of plates and walked into the kitchen, hoping to end the ridiculous conversation. When he followed instead, she groaned out loud.

"All I'm saying is you should be more consistent with your opinions. You're sending mixed messages, and it's confusing.

She turned back from the sink, looked him directly in the eyes, and raised her brow. It took him a couple of seconds to realize his hypocrisy, but once he did, his cheeks reddened, and he walked away without another word. With a shake of her head, she turned back to the sink so she could load the dishwasher.

"That was...interesting," Molly said once the room had cleared and they were the only two left.

"What the heck was that even about?" Grace asked, exasperated. "I told you he took issue with my truck comments, but jeez, that felt a little extreme."

"That conversation had nothing to do with the truck and everything to do with Mr. Tall, Dark, and Handsome," said Molly, her eyebrows wiggling up and down. When she saw the confused look on Grace's face, she elaborated. "He's jealous!"

"Jealous of what?"

"Of Cole, duh. You sure are being pretty dense this morning."

"Gee, thanks," she said as she rolled her eyes. "He has no reason to be jealous; he has a girlfriend. A girlfriend who reminds everyone of that fact, including him, daily."

"Then why is he still here? No, scratch that; why did he even come back in the first place?"

Grace shrugged. "I'm not the only reason Hunter was planning to move here. I imagine he returned because of the new business he's supposed to set up with Grant. In case you haven't noticed, that's the one place he's been spending all his time."

"Oh, trust me, I've noticed. Especially since he started bringing her to work with him. Doesn't change the facts, though. And the facts say that he is jealous. I don't think he likes how fast you've moved on."

"That's rich, given he started dating Rebekah without breaking up with me first. Did you know he still hasn't officially broken up with me?" Grace shook her head in disgust. "Besides, while I have moved on from my relationship with Hunter, Cole and I are just friends."

Molly raised her brow in question. "You sure are spending a lot of time with him."

"I spend a lot of time with you too. Should I consider us a couple?"

Molly laughed. "Okay, fine, you win. Seriously though, I just want you to be happy. If there's a chance for you and Cole...," she trailed off.

"Cole and I agreed to take things slow. I have a lot of feelings to work through, and I imagine he doesn't want to risk becoming Mr. Rebound. I'm in no rush to jump into another relationship, especially with another man I barely know."

"Taking things slowly makes sense, but what will you do if Hunter chooses to stay here?"

"That depends. Is she staying with him?"

"No, she moves on."

"In that case, he can continue to rent his room. They will have to find somewhere else if she's staying, too. I'm not sure how much more I can take of her."

"And if he wants to pick up where he left off with you?" she asked gently.

Grace quickly shook her head. "That will not be happening. Relationships require trust, and after the way Hunter handled things, I will never be able to fully trust him again." She wiped down the counters and pulled out her recipe book. "Not that any of this matters anyway. I'm confident he will follow Rebekah back to New York."

"Maybe," Molly looked unsure. "Anyway, I have some updates to give you."

Grace looked up from the dessert section. "I hope they're good updates."

"I talked to Grant, and we agreed that while it might be unconventional, we will allow it if Emilio still wants to stay here. Grant thinks that observing him in an informal setting will give him better insight into the guy's personality."

"That makes sense. How did Emilio feel about it? As my guest, I don't want him to feel like he has to be 'on' all weekend. It will ruin the experience for him."

"Surprisingly, he was excited about it. He reminded me that interviews are a two-way street and said he's interested in seeing how Grant interacts with people outside of business hours. So, his reservation has been confirmed and paid in full."

"That's great news. Did Vanessa follow through on her reservation as well?"

"Yep, she paid the same day. Which brings us to Jane. I ended up sending her the booking information. With only a few days left, I didn't want to risk the room remaining empty."

Grace nodded. "It's going to be an interesting group of people. I just hope Rebekah doesn't ruin things by continuing her endless campaign of convincing us all she and Hunter are soulmates."

Molly sighed. "Grant has already had to speak to Hunter once about asking her to tone it down at the office. We may have to talk with Hunter as well."

"That has awkward written all over it," Grace replied dryly. "If I ask him to rein her in, he'll just accuse me of jealousy."

"I'll ask Grant to talk to him again. I'm sure he won't mind; if he does, he'll likely just do it anyway. I hate to say it, but many of us will feel a sense of relief when the two of them finally leave.

"I know I will. At least when she leaves. I told you letting her stay here would be a mistake."

"Yes, and you were right, but what was I supposed to do? Tell her no?"

"That's exactly what you were supposed to do. You could have said we're already fully booked. She had no way of knowing whether or not that was true."

"In my defense, I had no idea any of this would happen."

Grace shrugged again. "There's no point in arguing; what's done is done. I just hope she leaves when she says she will. Anyway, do you have any other updates?"

"We've sold over eight hundred tickets to the murder mystery dinner!"

"Wow! We might actually reach a thousand sales," Grace said, surprised at the new information. "I hope we bought enough supplies."

"I'm sure we'll be fine. I thought you'd be a lot more excited about this," Molly said, disappointed.

"You're not the one who has to do an insane amount of cooking," Grace quipped. "Honestly, though, I am excited; I'm just a little overwhelmed by the number of people coming through my home. This place is also a business, but it's been my home for over twenty years. Opening it up to the public like this will take some time to get used to."

"I can understand that. You're so good at being a hostess, I sometimes forget just how new to this you are."

"I'll take that as a compliment."

"It was meant as one," Molly smiled. "

Thank you," Grace smiled back. "What about the event we're hosting on Valentine's Day? I feel like I've dropped the ball where that's concerned, and I'm starting to panic at the thought the day will come and we'll end up with a bunch of disappointed and angry people."

"No need to panic; I've already done most of the work. I've lined up about a dozen big ticket items for the auction, booked a DJ, and there's a committee already formed of people who will be on decorating duty for the big event. All that's left are the food and drinks, which I believe Bea, Addie, Cole, and you will handle as soon as we get past the mystery dinner."

"Okay," Grace said, letting out a sigh of relief. "It sounds like you have things under control. I'm not sure what I'd do without you."

"Likewise, sister!" Molly checked her phone. "I guess I better head to the office."

"You're welcome to work here if you'd prefer. I'm about to start baking again and always need taste testers."

"You know what? That sounds like a great idea. I'll go get my laptop out of the car and set up over there at the dining table."

Grace nodded, then set to work picking out her next recipe. The window of time before her next group of guests arrived was slowly closing, and she felt the pressure. It was a good thing there were two solid months between now and the next holiday. She would need every second to recover.

-Days till Valentine's Day-

Four

"Today's the big day," Grace announced at breakfast Friday morning. "Our newest group of guests will arrive sometime this afternoon."

"Do you need help getting things ready?" Molly asked as she sipped her cup of tea. Her morning appetite seemed to have decreased as of late, and Grace suspected morning sickness had set in.

"I think I have everything under control. I just need to do a quick once-over in the bedrooms and clean the bathrooms. Shouldn't take too long."

"If you change your mind, let me know. I plan to work from home again today, so I'll be around if you need me."

Grace nodded in understanding. "I heard from Carl. He's decided to take Katherine and Edward up on their offer to move back home. He'd like to come by for a few days next month before he moves, and of course, I agreed."

"Who's Carl?" asked Rebekah.

"He was one of the guests that stayed here over Christmas," Hunter explained. "Grace was instrumental in reconnecting him with his estranged siblings, and from the sound of things, it's going pretty well for them," he beamed at her, the first sign of the old Hunter she had seen since he'd returned.

"I see," Rebekah said, clearly annoyed. "You seem to have men everywhere, don't you?"

"One can never have too many admirers," Grace responded dryly. "Anyway, it will be nice to see him again."

"Yes, it will," Molly mused. "It's nice he's stayed in touch. Have you heard from anyone else?"

Grace shook her head. "No, but I didn't expect to. Carl was the only one I formed any kind of relationship with. I imagine it will be like that with most of our guests." It took a lot of effort to avoid looking at Rebekah when she said the last part. She could only hope Rebekah would be one of the ones on the list of guests she'd never see again.

"Do you know when Emilio is supposed to arrive?" asked Grant. "I would like to come by and introduce myself. Maybe take him out for a drink or two."

"All he could tell me is he planned to be here before dinner. I can text you when he arrives if you'd like?"

"That would be great. Thank you, Grace." Grant stood up and kissed Molly on the cheek. "I'm off to the office. See you all later," he said before exiting the room. He appeared to be in a hurry, but that could have just been her imagination.

Taking that as her cue, she stood up and cleared the dishes. She had a long list of things she needed to do today;

the sooner she started working on them, the better chance she had of actually getting them all done.

"You know, you don't have to include meals," said Rebekah as she watched her stack the plates. "Breakfast is obviously expected, but the rest is usually the guests' responsibility. At least at all the places I've stayed..."

"Yes, I know, but there are very few restaurants around here. I aim to make our guest's stay here as convenient as possible."

Rebekah shrugged. She looked like she planned to say more but ultimately changed her mind. "Hunter, are you ready to go?" she asked instead.

"Yes, I just need a minute with Grace. Do you mind waiting for me in the car?" he asked.

If the look on her face was any indication, she very much minded but seemed unable to come up with a good enough reason to object. Instead, she stood up in a huff and flounced away from the table.

"You're going to pay for that," Molly laughed. "I'm going to get these two settled while you talk," she waved her hand toward Granny and Gladys, who had been strangely silent that morning.

After they cleared the room, an ordeal that took several minutes due to the snail-like pace at which Granny and Gladys moved, Grace took a deep breath and turned to face Hunter. "What's up?"

"Grant talked with me last night about Rebekah. He relayed some of your concerns regarding her meal-time behavior. Specifically, her constant need to discuss the relationship between her and me."

Grace nodded. "This time around, we're doing a reverse holiday celebration. Our guests are coming because they want to avoid the very behavior Rebekah keeps displaying. So, it would be awesome if you could please make her stop."

"Isn't that your job, as the owner of this place?" he asked, clearly nervous about the topic of conversation.

"If she were my guest, discussing her behavior would fall on me. Unfortunately, she isn't here as my guest; she's here as your girlfriend. More importantly, the only reason she feels the need to act that way in the first place is because you failed to be honest with her, and now she feels insecure."

Hunter was silent momentarily, no doubt processing what she had just said. "Wait a minute," he said at last. "Are you saying she knows about us?"

"Duh! Did you think it was just a coincidence she started acting clingy and loudly proclaiming your love to anyone who would listen right after we had that talk the other day?"

"She overheard us?" he asked. His face went pale, little beads of sweat forming on his temples.

"Yes, Hunter, she overheard us. But don't worry, I did my best to reassure her that I'm not a threat to your relationship. It appears I may have failed, but I did try."

"Look, I'm sorry, but there's nothing I can do. Rebekah has a mind of her own, and if I try to say something, especially now, she'll accuse me of caring more about you than I do her."

"Then leave."

"What?"

"You heard me. We both know you're going to leave, anyway. The only reason she's here is because of you. So, if you return to New York, she will follow."

"I'm not ready to leave," he said, shaking his head. "I'm still trying to figure out my business with Grant and what I want to do..."

"Look, you're going to have to pick one. You know how important this bed-and-breakfast is to me, and it isn't fair to make me live under constant threat of losing it all because your girlfriend has decided to blame me for the mess you created."

"You're being a little dramatic. A few displays of affection in front of your guests will not ruin your business."

"That's not the only threat I'm referring to. Every time I fail to live up to her expectations, she pulls out her phone and threatens to post about her 'horrible' experience on all her social media accounts. Honestly, Hunter. I realize she's beautiful and has an air of sophistication about her few will ever possess, but..." Grace trailed off as the realization of what she was saying hit.

"I know," he said, running his hand through his hair. "It's not entirely her fault, though. She's so used to getting what she wants, to have never heard the word no; she doesn't know how to handle it on the rare occasions it does happen."

"You're not doing her any favors by becoming one of her 'yes men.'"

"No, I suppose not. I'm just not sure how... I'll try, okay? It's the best I can do."

"You know, there have been times when I wondered if you have a twin you swapped places with when you went back to New York. Because the Hunter that returned to Winterwood is the opposite of the one that left after Christmas." Grace shook her head. "I hope you find what you're looking for. And I hope you find it before I end up collateral damage."

Before he could respond, she turned on her heel and walked away. Tears of frustration burned her eyes, and she didn't want to risk him seeing them for fear he would misunderstand their meaning. She wasn't sure which Hunter was the 'real' Hunter or if neither were. All she knew was the man she had previously fallen for was gone.

***

A knock at the door startled Grace, and she dropped the piping bag she had been using. Since it was the first night of her guests' stay, she had spent a good portion of her day creating a variety of fancy desserts she hoped would impress. After a quick rinse of her sticky hands, she went to the door and discovered a well-dressed man of Latino descent standing on her porch. "You must be Emilio," she said, extending her hand. "Welcome to Winterwood!"

"Thank you. It's a pleasure to be here," he said, shaking her extended hand in greeting.

"Please, come in; I'll show you to your room," she waved him inside, shutting the door behind him.

"Oh wow, the molding in here is beautiful," he said, his neck craned back as he looked up toward the ceiling. "French-inspired?"

"Yes, it is. You know your architecture," she led him up the stairs.

"I'll have to admit, it's my first love. But architecture is a difficult field to get into, and opportunities to create something like this," he said, waving his hand toward the intricately carved details. "Don't seem to exist these days."

"You're right. I've never heard of someone building a modern-day Sistine Chapel. It's a real shame," she replied, a sense of pride washing over her. America was too young of a country to compete in the historical architecture department, but she took pride in the knowledge her house qualified as a monument to the past. "Is that why you chose to go into finance? More opportunities?"

"While it comes in a distant second, finance is my second love," he gasped when she opened the door to his room and led him inside. "This room is amazing! It even has its own fireplace!"

Grace smiled at his enthusiasm. It was always interesting to see her home through the eyes of others. It gave her a new appreciation for things she usually took for granted. "I'm glad you like it. The bathroom is across the hall, and my room is at the end if you need anything. I'll give you some time to get settled. When you're ready, I'll give you a tour."

She turned to leave but stopped when he called out her name. "Can I ask you a question before you leave?" he asked, somewhat hesitantly.

"Of course."

"What can you tell me about Grant?"

"Oh, well, I don't know him professionally, but personally, he's a really nice guy. Always ready to lend a hand when needed, and more importantly, does so with a good attitude. He's very serious about his business, but I believe he's a fair man."

"It's just, I drove around a little bit before I got here, and this town is...not what I expected."

"You're wondering why he decided to open a finance company in a town the size of a postage stamp?"

Emilio laughed. "Not to be rude, but that's exactly what I'm wondering. I'm looking for an opportunity to grow in my career, and from what I've seen, this might not be it."

"To be honest, I have zero experience in the corporate world, so I am probably not the best one to address your concerns. I'll tell you this, though: Grant was a successful businessman in Boston before he moved here to open his own finance company. He came here because his wife has family, and he hoped to establish a more balanced work-life ratio."

Emilio nodded at her explanation. "That seems reasonable. The cost of living is likely much lower here, which would be beneficial."

"Moving here, especially from a place like Texas, can be challenging. My advice is to talk to Grant about your concerns. The last thing you want is to accept a job here and end up miserable."

"I just don't want to come off as snobby or rude. Job interviews are a two-way street, but I still need to uphold my end of the value proposition."

"Grant is going through everything you will should you end up here. If he is unwilling to address your concerns for some reason, I would consider that a red flag."

"Okay, you're right. Thanks."

"No problem. I know he wants to stop by and introduce himself. That might be a good time to talk about some of the things you're worried about."

"That sounds like a great idea," he looked around the room again and smiled. "I have a good feeling about this."

"I'm glad to hear that," she replied; a knock on the door halted further discussion. "Excuse me, I think that might be another guest."

Grace left the room and hurried down the stairs. When she opened the door, a tall woman with purple hair greeted her enthusiastically.

"You must be Grace," she said, extending her hand. "I'm so excited to finally be here!"

"Vanessa?" she asked, hopeful she was right.

"That's me," she replied cheerfully.

Grace let out a little sigh of relief. "Come on in; I'll show you to your room."

"Sorry if I'm a little early. I heard it's supposed to snow tonight, and I didn't want to get caught in it if it decided to show up early."

"I heard about that too, and you're not early. In fact, one of our other guests arrived about fifteen minutes before you."

"Oh good," she stopped talking when she saw her room.

Grace had done a little redecorating over the last few weeks and given this room, particularly, a much-needed makeover. As one of the smaller rooms, she needed to find a way to make it feel special, so she added a canopy over the bed and swapped the chairs for a fainting couch in front of the fireplace. In her opinion, the room looked like something out of a historical Regency novel. You know, the kind about members of the nobility? Minus the size, of course.

"This room is absolutely amazing," Vanessa said somewhat breathlessly. "I may never leave!"

"I'm so glad to hear that. This is my favorite room in the house, so it's nice to see someone shares my rather biased opinion," Grace laughed.

Another knock on the door heralded the arrival of their last guest. "Excuse me, I need to get that. We'll be having cocktails around five thirty with dinner at six. Feel free to come down whenever you're ready."

Grace left the room and closed the door behind her. Only one more to go, and she had to admit, this was the one she was most interested in meeting, if only to see if her preconceived notions were correct. When she opened the door, she was greeted by a woman wearing sweatpants and oversized glasses. Her straight, brown hair was in a messy bun, and her face was completely devoid of makeup.

"You must be Jane," Grace smiled. "Welcome to Winterwood!"

"Thank you," Jane replied curtly. "I trust that I'm on time?"

"Of course. Please come in, and I'll show you to your room."

Jane followed her up the stairs and into her room without comment. Once inside, she looked around and dumped her bags on the bed unceremoniously. "I suppose this will do."

Grace was more than a little taken aback by her attitude. Even Rebekah had been excited about her room, and Grace was pretty sure she stayed in places at least ten times nicer on the regular. They should have listened to Molly's gut when she said she didn't think Jane would be a good fit. Oh well, too late now. She gave the dinner schedule then left as quickly as possible.

At least Emilio and Vanessa had seemed nice. Although, it's possible that Jane is also nice, just tired and cranky from the long drive. Yes, Grace chided herself; it's way too early to judge her. We'll just have to give her some time to rest and settle in, and then see how she is. She can't be any worse than Rebekah. Can she?

-Days till Valentine's Day-

Three

T he day of the Murder Mystery Dinner had finally arrived, but instead of excitement, Grace felt nothing but panic and dread. Word had gotten around town about Lula and Chrissy's offers, and the tiny streets of Winterwood had been flooded with shoppers since seven that morning. Grace knew because her phone had rang with complaints ever since. What the complainers thought she could do about it was anyone's guess, but she had tried her best. A quick call to Mayor Allen netted a couple of deputies for assistance.

While that helped with the traffic problem, it did little to solve the problem of too many people and not enough products to sell or workers to sell them. Bea's Bakery had sold out of every baked good she had to offer before eight, Lula was booked solid with a line of walk-ins down the street, and Chrissy, who didn't even open until ten, had so many people waiting to enter her shop, she was afraid to even open her doors. It was bad. Very, very bad. The worst part is Grace heavily suspected this turn-out was more about the free wine than the actual goods and services for sale.

The doorbell rang, the first time someone had used it, and Grace almost ran to the corner to hide; she was so afraid that people had taken to showing up at her door instead of calling. She gathered her courage and answered the door, only to find Cole on the other side instead of the angry mob she had imagined. "I'm so glad to see you," she said, the words rushing out of her mouth. "Unless you're here to complain. Are you here to complain? Please tell me you're not here to complain."

"Whoa, calm down," he said, grabbing her by the shoulders and giving her a little shake. "What's going on?"

Grace looked up at him, her eyes blinking in surprise. "I take it you haven't been downtown this morning?"

"No, why? What's going on downtown?"

She told him all about it, down to the last nitty-gritty detail. By the time she was finished, she was so out of breath from talking so fast she was practically hyperventilating.

"I can see why this is a problem, but why is it such a big deal to you?"

"I've already scheduled appointments for my guests to visit these places later today. It was supposed to be a fun, relaxing way to spend the day before the murder mystery dinner. I'm terrified that not only will they have a horrible time, what with all the crowds, but Chrissy will sell out long before they can get there. My guests already paid for this experience, Cole. They're going to be angry if it ends up being awful," she replied, her breathing somewhat ragged. The more she voiced her fears, the more panicked she became.

Cole moved his hand from her shoulder to her face, bent down, and kissed her. When they pulled apart, she looked up at him with wide eyes. "What was that for?"

"To help you calm down. It was either kiss you or slap you," he shrugged. "I'd never hit a woman, so...."

"You really thought kissing me would help me calm down?" she asked incredulously. "I'm pretty sure my heart is racing twice as fast as before."

He pulled her up against him and began to rub slow circles against her back with the palm of his hand. It took a while, but she eventually felt herself relax against him. "Feel better now?" he asked, his lips against her ear.

Afraid to speak and break the spell, she nodded. When he let go, she pulled him back, not yet ready to leave the safety of his arms. After a few more minutes of clinging to him, she finally let go. "Thank you," she sighed. "Now, what can I do for you?"

"Actually, I'm here to help you."

"Me? So you did know about the problems downtown?"

"No, I came to help you get ready for tonight. Which is what you should focus on. What's happening downtown is neither your problem nor your fault, and there's nothing you can do about it. So let's not let it derail your plans, okay?"

"But what about my guests and Lula and Chrissy?" Grace practically whined.

"Lula and Chrissy are responsible for their businesses. They know what they're supposed to do, so let them do it. If your guests have a bad experience, and at this point, that is still a big if, we will deal with it then."

"Okay," she replied hesitantly. "I guess you're right."

"Good," he said, taking her hand and leading her back inside. "On the bright side, the snow they predicted last night held off. At least we don't have to worry about that."

"Except they're expecting it tonight instead."

"Yeah, but not until after midnight. The event will be over long before then, so there shouldn't be any problems road-wise."

They walked into the kitchen; Cole's eyes widened at the sight. "It looks like I got here just in time," he said, letting out a low whistle. "When you go crazy, you really go crazy!"

Grace surveyed the scene of the chaos thoughtfully. It looked like a tornado had come through and sprayed flour everywhere. It was embarrassing. "It's been a rough morning," she finally said.

"Do you have a list of what you need to complete before tonight?"

"Yeah, it's on the counter," she said, pointing to the far end of the kitchen.

He walked over, picked up the sheet of paper, and studied it momentarily. "Okay, let's start at the top and work our way down."

A sense of relief washed over her. She wasn't alone. "Thanks, Cole."

"No problem," he grinned. "Maybe someday you'll return the favor!"

She couldn't imagine what that would look like. She had zero bartending experience, so he couldn't be referring to that. Maybe she could help feed his cows sometime. That was something she was confident she could do.

***

It was finally time for the event to start. Grace and Cole had spent the entire day cooking, baking, and setting up their serving station. Now, it was time for the fun to begin.

While shopping at party stores the other day, they stumbled upon some old-fashioned bartender and bar-maid costumes and decided it would be fun to dress the part. They looked like they belonged in an old English pub, but Grace felt that was close enough. People would know what they were, and that was all that mattered.

"Okay, everyone," Grace said, addressing the guests hanging out in the living room. "The event starts at the park. Mayor Allen will kick things off with a little back-story and give you your first clue. Grant," she said, pointing to him, "Will lead you over there."

Everyone, including Rebekah and Hunter, followed Grant out the door. "I thought Rebekah said this would be 'hokey,'" Grace whispered to Molly.

"She did, but then she posted about it on her socials. Instead of everyone agreeing with her on how lame it sounded, they posted comments about how much fun it sounded and how they wished they could go, too. She changed her tune pretty fast once that happened."

Grace shook her head. "The power of social media..."

Molly laughed. "Sometimes it works in your favor."

"Sometimes. Until it doesn't." Deciding to let the conversation drop, she walked to Granny's room and peeked her head in. "Are you ladies ready for your acting debut?"

"Ready as we'll ever be," Granny replied.

"Do I look dead enough?" Gladys asked.

Grace moved closer to get a better look. "More dead than I'm comfortable with," she replied. "You just remember this is all an act," she wagged her finger at Gladys.

"Yes, ma'am," Gladys saluted.

"Remember, no moving when the people are in here. Even if Granny says something outrageous."

"I'll do my best. Heck, at my age, I'll probably end up falling asleep!"

"I'll make sure to nudge her if she gets out of line," Granny said, a mischievous smile on her face.

Grace laughed and then turned to go back to the kitchen. There were three locations with food for the mystery diners to go to, plus four without, though they were not in any given order. Which meant they could show up at any time. The last count Molly gave showed nine hundred and seventy-five tickets had been sold, though it was still possible for people to buy tickets 'at the gate,' so to speak.

When the guests arrived back at the house from their afternoon outing, all of them, including Jane, were smiling and laughing. Each one also had a new outfit and appeared relaxed and happy. So Grace had apparently freaked out for nothing. Something Cole had no problem pointing out to her. She would have been annoyed if she hadn't been so relieved to see her worst fears had been avoided. Memories of his kiss didn't hurt either. Not that she would admit that to him.

As the evening progressed, people trailed in and out, usually in groups and often more than a little tipsy. Everyone appeared to be in good spirits and raved about her food. Some even took the time to compliment their costumes, many assuming they were a couple. That part had been a little embarrassing, but after a while, she decided to just take it as a compliment. If people were willing to assume that a guy like Cole was interested in a girl like her, who was she to argue?

Granny and Gladys had a blast entertaining the mystery solvers. Each time a group came through, Granny's story became more outrageous and, therefore, hysterical to listen to. Grace tried to rein her in but eventually gave up. As long as the facts remained the same, everyone had the same chance to solve the mystery. In the end, that was all that mattered.

After all of the mystery-solvers had a chance to visit all of the sites and an opportunity to return and ask follow-up questions, they were to return to the park. There were three suspects presented as the possible killers. A separate, giant container had been set up for each killer, and the mystery solvers were to place their tickets in the container of the killer they suspected. Once everyone had a chance to do that, Mayor Allen would finish the story and reveal the killer.

A drawing would then take place from the killer's container, and someone would win a prize. Grace wasn't sure what the prize was, as it hadn't been part of her job to come up with one, but she heard rumors that it was a spa package similar to the one she had set up for her guests.

It was close to midnight by the time it was over. Grace was exhausted but still had to make and serve breakfast in the morning, so she had no choice but to clean up now.

"Are you sure we can't put this off till tomorrow?" Cole asked. He looked equally exhausted, which was strange since this was pretty close to a typical night for him.

"Unfortunately, I can't. If I don't clean up now, my guests won't have anywhere to sit in the morning. You can go, though; you've done more than your share of work for the day."

Cole grinned. "And leave you here to clean all by your lonesome? That wouldn't be very chivalrous of me now, would it?"

She bumped his shoulder with hers. "Seriously. You still have chores to deal with in the morning. I have a feeling my guests will sleep in a little later than usual."

"Would you leave me?"

She thought about it for a minute. "No, I wouldn't. But again, I'm not the one who has to get up so early," she said, smiling at him. She had only meant to show him she was serious and wouldn't be mad if he left, but as she looked up into his eyes, something in the air shifted, the atmosphere now tinged with electricity as lightning bolts sizzled between them.

He bent his head, and this time she met him halfway, eager to experience his kiss again. Only this time, it wasn't just a chaste kiss to distract her from panicking; it was a 'make you forget your own name' swoon-worthy kiss. The kind that if he hadn't been holding on to her, she might have actually swooned. She would have gladly stayed in his arms forever, but the sound of someone clearing their throat finally broke them apart.

Cole was the first to react to the intrusion, his body tense in her arms. Still holding on to him, she turned her head to see who was causing all the tension, her body stiffening when she saw Hunter and Rebekah standing in the doorway. The way they looked at them was almost comical, their expressions so different it was as if they were staring at two different things. Hunter's gaze was angry and accusatory, Rebekah's smug and triumphant.

"Looks like I should have believed you when you told me I had nothing to worry about," Rebekah said snarkily. "You really do have men all over the place."

She was sure she would have come up with the perfect come-back if her mind wasn't still addled from the heart-stopping kiss. But alas, it was not to be. So, she had to settle for killing her with kindness instead. "Is there something I can do for you?" Grace asked sweetly.

"Looks like you've got your hands full in here," Hunter replied icily. "We were going to see if you need help cleaning up, but you seem to have everything under control.

Let's go, Rebekah," he said, grabbing her hand and yanking her toward the stairs.

Cole and Grace watched them go. "Are you okay?" he finally asked.

She looked up at him. "No," she replied. When she saw the hurt flash across his face, she quickly added. "They interrupted my fairy-tale moment."

"Oh yeah?" he said, raising his brow. "How's that?"

She wrapped her arms around his neck and pulled his mouth down to hers. "The princess was busy kissing her prince," she said, closing the distance between their lips.

Minutes later, or hours for all she knew, her sense of time out the window long ago, Cole broke apart from her. "If we're not careful," he said when she made a sound of protest, "Cinderella will turn back into a pumpkin."

"That's not how that works," she laughed. "But I know what you mean. It's time for you to head on home."

"Let's just get things cleaned up real quick, and then we can both go to bed. Separately," he said when she gave him a questioning look.

"Okay, fine, but don't get mad at me when you wake up dead tired in the morning."

"Never!"

Since they decided to work together, it took less time than Grace had estimated to get the kitchen back into a functioning state. Once they were done, she helped Cole load the unused supplies into the back of his truck, both sighing in relief when they were finally done. As they said goodbye, snow flurries began to fall from the sky, swirling around them like dancing fairies.

"Maybe this really is a fairy tale," he said as he gently brushed a snowflake off her cheek.

"If it is, I hope it's one with a happy ending."

"Don't they all have happy endings?"

She shook her head sadly. "No, not all of them."

He bent down and kissed her cheek where the snowflake had just been. "Goodnight, Grace."

"Goodnight, Cole."

He got in his truck and started the engine, waving one last time before he drove away. She remained on the porch long after he'd gone, watching the snow fall. Regardless of what happened between her and Cole, she would treasure this night for the rest of her life.

-Days till Valentine's Day-

Two

G race awoke to the sound of her alarm clock. It was five-thirty in the morning, and as she lay there in her nice, warm bed, she contemplated the events of the night before and what had ultimately led to her waking up so early. After Cole had left and still on a high from all his kisses, she decided to get up and help him with his chores, thus returning the favor he had done for her the day before. It had seemed like a good idea at the time, but now, in the not-so-light of day, she regretted her decision.

What if she drove there only to discover he had decided to sleep in? Or what if he got up earlier than she thought? Did she really want to wander around his farm in the cold and snow looking for him? On the other hand, he stayed late last night to help her clean up. So, helping him with his chores was the right thing to do.

Her decision made; she got up, her tired body groaning in protest, and dressed in her warmest clothes. That done, she walked as silently as possible past the bedrooms in the hallway, expertly navigated the creaky stairs, and slipped out through the back door. Thankfully, while it had snowed, there was less than an inch on the ground. Any more, and she would have been forced to delay her plan, her small car no match for unpaved roads.

It was still dark out, so she drove slowly, simultaneously watching the road and the clock on her dashboard. If she had any chance of catching him, she needed to get there before six. At five-fifty, she finally pulled onto his drive and started down the long, winding lane. At five fifty-two, she pulled up to his house and sighed in relief when she saw the light in the kitchen and his truck parked in the drive. Then she remembered he drove that mule thing when he did his chores.

Oh well, she thought, I'm here, so I might as well see if I'm too late. She exited her car and walked up to the porch, the door opening right as she raised her hand to knock.

"Grace!" he called out in surprise. "What are you doing here? You about scared me half to death."

"Sorry about that," she said sheepishly. "I came to help you with your chores." Suddenly embarrassed, she looked down at the ground while she waited for his response.

"You came all the way out here, in the snow, to help with my chores?" he asked, confused. "Did we make plans I forgot about in my sleep-deprived state?"

"No," she said, shaking her head, her eyes still on the ground. This was not at all going the way she thought it would.

"Why don't you come inside? It's freezing out there."

Was it freezing? She didn't feel cold. In fact, she felt warm, her face flushed with embarrassment. She was tempted to turn around and run back to the safety of her car but managed to soldier on and follow him inside.

"Coffee?" he asked.

She nodded in response, her voice no longer working. This had been a foolish idea. Obviously, she had read way too much into his feelings the night before and was making a big fool of herself. And to think, she could have just stayed in bed and gotten some much-needed sleep.

A minute later, he returned with two cups, handing one of them to her. "Sit," he ordered.

Too overcome with emotion to object, she sat on the couch, her eyes focused on her coffee cup. Movement flashed in the corner of her eye, and the next thing she knew, Max was at her side, his big head in her lap. She gave the big beast of a dog a small smile and pet his head, laughing a little when his tail started thumping in enthusiasm.

"So what's this about you helping with my chores?" Cole asked, breaking the uncomfortable silence.

Still unwilling to meet his gaze, she focused on the dog. "After you left last night, I looked at the time and saw how late it was. I felt bad you would have to get up so early, so I thought if I came and helped you, just like you helped me, you would get done faster."

"Do you know what I do this early in the morning?"

Grace shrugged. "No."

"Yet, you came anyway?"

"I figured it couldn't be that bad. And even if it was, two people should still be better than one."

She heard him get up from his chair and watched from the corner of her eye as he moved to sit beside her on the couch. When he reached over and took the cup from her hand, she let go and watched him set it on the coffee table in front of them. Surprised when he reached for her hand and clasped it in his, she finally looked up at him.

"That is probably the nicest thing anyone has ever done for me," he said, staring into her eyes.

"It's nothing you wouldn't do for me," she replied.

"I'm sure I don't need to remind you that you got just as little sleep as I did?"

"No," she replied, shaking her head. "I am well aware of how little sleep I got."

He chuckled as he pulled her close to him. "Are you sure you want to do this?"

She nodded up at him, afraid if she spoke, it would give away the fact she really wasn't sure at all. He was starting to make her nervous. Were they about to spend the next couple of hours mucking out horse stalls? Could she handle it if they were?

"Alright," he said, kissing the tip of her nose. "Let's go see what you're made of."

Okay, now she was really scared. Her initial plan had been to help him feed hay to some cows. Obviously, his chores involved quite a bit more than that. Hopefully, she didn't end up regretting this. What's that saying again? No good deed goes unpunished?

***

It was ten o'clock by the time Grace got home. When she realized the chores would take longer than expected, she texted Molly and asked her to cover for her at breakfast. Molly had agreed with the caveat that Grace relay every last detail of her latest adventure and begrudgingly agreed.

Once inside, she met Molly in the kitchen.

"Eww, you smell like a cow," Molly exclaimed, holding her nose with her thumb and forefinger.

"Guess that means you'll want to hold off your interrogation until after I've showered?" Grace asked, although it was more of a statement than a question.

"Yes, please go shower. I'll be in the dining room when you're done."

Grace saluted and then took off for her bedroom, using the servants' stairs to avoid running into her guests. When she got out of the shower, she checked her phone and saw she had a message from Cole, 'Thanks so much for helping out this morning. You're the best!' It wasn't exactly a declaration of love and devotion, but she'd take it. She texted back the thumbs-up emoji and hurried to get dressed. Today was supposed to be game day with the guests, and she felt the need to make herself available even though all she wanted was to climb back into bed and sleep for the rest of the month.

Back downstairs, Molly cornered her in the kitchen. "So, give me all the juicy details," Molly demanded.

"I'm not sure what kind of juicy details you're expecting, but I fear I'm about to disappoint. All I did was help Cole with his farm chores this morning. Chores that consisted of shoveling horse poop, hauling hay and water out to the pastures for the cows, and fixing a section of electric fence that had come loose when a branch fell on it."

"That's it?"

"I'm afraid so. I seriously wish I had more to report, but by the time we were done, we were both so tired I simply waved goodbye, got back in my car, and came home."

"Huh," she said, crinkling her nose. "Next time you go sneaking out late at night, make sure it's for a better reason than horse manure."

"I'll do my best. Not to change the subject, but have you seen Hunter and Rebekah this morning?"

"No, neither of them have come down yet; why?"

"There was an...incident last night, and I hope to avoid them. Which is stupid given how unlikely that is."

"Ooh, so there is something juicy to tell. Spill it, sister!"

Grace sighed. "They walked in on Cole and me kissing."

Molly raised her brows. "And how did that go?"

"Not well. Rebekah looked like she'd just won the lottery, but Hunter was angry. His eyes practically shot daggers at me, and he acted like he'd just walked in on me cheating on him or something."

"I'm sure in his mind he did," Molly said, compassion in her voice.

"Which one of us are you feeling sorry for?" Grace asked. "Him, for watching the woman he ghosted move on with her life? Or me, for having to put up with the jealousy of the guy who ghosted me in favor of someone else?"

"My loyalty is to you, of course," Molly assured Grace. "It's just, I'm sure it hurt to see you with someone else. Even though he's a jerk, he still cares about you."

"He has a funny way of showing it," she said dryly. "I was willing to accept his decision and have tried to be happy for him despite what he put me through. Why can't he do the same for me?"

"Because a part of him still wants to be with you."

"He can't have it both ways."

"No, he can't. But feelings often aren't fair or logical."

Footsteps sounded on the stairs, the guests filing into the dining room one by one.

"What's on the agenda for today?" Vanessa asked.

"I thought you might be tired after all the excitement yesterday, so I planned a low-key, relaxing game day. I have plenty of board games to choose from, as well as puzzles and books for those who don't want to play."

Vanessa walked over to the game cabinet and looked through the selection. After a few minutes, she pulled a box out of the cabinet and turned back to face the group. "How about Pictionary? If we split up into groups of four, we can have an old-fashioned showdown!"

Grace looked around the room. "Does that sound good to everyone?"

They all nodded, Rebekah and Hunter included, although he had studiously avoided her since he came down.

"Okay then, I will grab some chips and dip while Molly gets Grant. Anyone want anything else?"

"Do you have more mini quiches from last night?" asked Emilio.

"I'm sure I do. Let me check, and if I find some, I'll heat them up and bring them out. Anything else?"

"What about those tarts?" Rebekah surprised her by asking. Grace had made numerous desserts for her, and she had claimed to hate every single one until now. Maybe Rebekah catching her with Cole had been a good thing after all.

"I'll grab some of those as well."

Grace assembled their requested snacks as the rest of the group gathered in the living room. When her phone dinged, she pulled it out of her pocket and saw Cole had sent another message. 'Just went through the inventory. Used more than expected. Going to need to make another trip to the city for supplies.'

Grace sighed; she had been afraid of that. Even worse, she had no idea if enough time had passed for the stores to restock their inventory. They might have to make the two-hour drive after all. 'Tomorrow work for you?' she texted back.

A few seconds later, her phone dinged again. 'Yes, any chance you want to help me with the chores first? My usual helper is out of town.' She really wanted to say no but felt obligated to say yes. After all, he was once again doing her a favor. 'Sure, same time?' she texted back, making a face. 'Yep, thanks!' Once again, she texted back the thumbs-up emoji.

At least this time, she would know what to expect. When Grant and Molly returned, she informed them of the latest development. "Can you take care of things for me tomorrow?" she asked Molly.

"Of course, just make sure you shower before getting in the truck with Cole."

"I'll consider it. Maybe he likes the smell of horse poop!"

Molly bumped her shoulder. "Come on, let's give these people a run for their money!"

They split into teams: Molly, Grant, Grace, and Jane on one, Hunter, Rebekah, Vanessa, and Emilio on the other. Grace wasn't sure, but she thought she might have seen a few sparks fly between Vanessa and Emilio. It wouldn't be the first time a miracle occurred at the bed-and-breakfast. If she were lucky, she could add matchmaker to her growing list of achievements.

-Days till Valentine's Day-

One

As promised, Grace had gone to Cole's farm and helped him with his morning chores. To get things done faster, she suggested they split up. Since she couldn't drive a tractor, that meant she got stuck shoveling the horse poop. No good deed really did go unpunished.

To both of their surprise, she was done by the time he returned from the pasture. To her surprise only, Cole seemed less than impressed. In fact, he was in a downright foul mood. Unsure of what to do with him, she left to go home and shower. They had agreed he would pick her up around ten, but given his mood, she wasn't sure he would show.

Still, she did her part and was ready and waiting long before the agreed-upon time. Since she finally had some time to spare, she headed to Granny's room to spend time with her. "Hi, Stranger!" she said as she entered the room.

"Well, hello, dear. It feels like I haven't seen you in ages!"

"I know; I hope you don't feel I've neglected you. I've just been so busy..."

"I know that, dear, and I don't blame you one bit. If anything, I'm incredibly grateful for all you do to keep this old gal running. Me and the house!"

"Oh, Granny," Grace laughed. "I'm happy to take care of both of you. Although, I can't help but look forward to some downtime."

Granny reached out and took Grace's hand in hers. "I'm looking forward to that, too. It's nice to have guests occasionally, but it will be nice when things return to normal."

"It's funny," Grace said. "For years now, whenever it was just us, I would dream of a family big enough to fill our dining room table. Now that it's full, I long for the days when it was just us."

"Most of them aren't real family," she said, patting her hand. "I've done my best to remain silent, but I know these last couple of weeks with Hunter and that woman haven't been easy for you."

Grace took a deep breath and let it out slowly. "No, they haven't. But I don't think those two are the only problem. Although it will help when they pack up and return to New York."

"Even Hunter?" Granny asked gently.

"Even Hunter." Grace heard her phone ding and checked to see Cole had texted he was outside. She made a face. "Duty calls, I'm afraid."

"Thanks for taking the little time you have to see me."

"Please don't act like I'm doing you a favor. I've missed you terribly and am just as thankful for these moments," she said, bending down to hug Granny. "Molly and Gladys are on their way over, so don't worry about being alone, okay?"

Granny nodded. "Of course, dear, I had no doubt you'd take care of me."

"I love you, Granny."

"I love you too."

Grace waved goodbye one more time and then left, her heart heavy. Once inside Cole's truck, she quickly discovered his mood had not improved and debated what to do. Remembering how he had handled her the other day, she turned to face him. "Out with it," she said calmly yet sternly.

"Excuse me?" he growled.

"You heard me. Tell me what's put you in such a bad mood. Real friends tell the truth, remember?"

He glanced at her long enough to give her a quick glare and then turned his attention back to the road. "I don't appreciate you using my words against me."

"I didn't appreciate it when you used them on me either, so too bad," she shot back.

He took a deep breath and sighed. "Fine, have it your way. You've helped me with chores twice now, and you didn't complain even once. Also, we agreed to take things slow. Can't help but notice we've been breaking that rule."

"Did you seriously just tell me you're mad at me because I didn't complain about helping you?" she asked incredulously. "What kind of foolishness is that?"

"I feel like you're being disingenuous," he said petulantly. "Any normal woman would complain about shoveling manure."

"Choosing not to complain about something that sucks does not make me disingenuous; it makes me someone with a good attitude. The work needed to be done, so I did it. Complaining would not have accomplished anything. As for taking things slow, if you don't want to kiss me again, then fine, don't kiss me." She crossed her arms over her chest and turned away from him. Now, they were both mad. Which was not the outcome she had hoped for.

They spent the rest of the drive in silence, both lost in their thoughts. When they pulled up to the first store, Grace grabbed her purse and moved to jump out of the truck, grateful for the opportunity to put some distance between them. When he grabbed her arm, she stopped to look back at him. "Yes?" she asked, her brow raised.

"Can we talk for a minute? Please?" he asked, the anger gone from his voice.

She was tempted to refuse but ultimately decided against it. They still had a long day ahead of them, and staying angry would only make a long trip that much longer. So she closed the door and sat back in her seat.

"I'm sorry," he said after a minute of silence. "I've been acting like a jerk, and you've done nothing to deserve that."

"I guess this means we're even then," she replied dryly. It took him a minute to realize why she said that, but when he did, he laughed. "Why are you so upset?" she asked again.

"I was married once," he admitted. He looked at her and saw the surprise on her face. "She was a lot like Hunter.

Grew up in a big city and loved the idea of marrying a cowboy and living on a ranch. In practice, she hated every minute of it. Complained incessantly about everything from how bad the poop smelled to how dirty the dirt was. God forbid I ask her for help either," he said, shaking his head.

"What happened?" Grace asked gently. She was tempted to reach over and touch his arm to comfort him, but his earlier comment about not taking things slow had hurt and made her feel her gesture would be unwelcome.

"Before we'd been married six months, I discovered she was cheating on me with some corporate dude up in the city. We were divorced before our first anniversary."

"Oh, Cole, I'm so sorry."

"I've been over her for a long time now, but I guess I still have some lingering feelings of distrust and maybe even resentment," he sighed. "When you volunteered to help me while simultaneously not complaining, it reminded me of her. Well, the exact opposite of her. It started to feel like maybe you were playing me too."

"I'm not sure what you mean by 'playing you,' but I can assure you, I was only trying to keep things even between us. You've done so much to help me lately; ironically, I was trying to ensure you didn't feel I was using you."

Cole snorted and shook his head. "You really are too good to be true, you know that?"

"I don't understand. Is that another insult?" she asked, confused.

He reached over and grabbed her, pulling her close to him. "No, darlin', that was not an insult," he said, cupping her face with his free hand and looking deep into her eyes.

When he moved to kiss her, she pulled her head back. "You told me you were angry we aren't taking things slow," she said accusingly.

"Hmm," he said, pulling her back to him and kissing her on her cheeks, nose, and forehead instead. "Did I say that?"

"Yes, you did," she said flatly. It was difficult to maintain her anger when he touched her like that, but what he said hurt, and she wasn't ready to let him off the hook so easily.

He finally noticed she was upset and stopped to look at her. "I'm sorry I said that; I didn't mean it. If anything, it feels like we're going too slow, but I know it's necessary for both our sakes. Will you forgive me? Please?" He made puppy dog faces at her, sticking out his bottom lip and batting his eyelashes.

Laughing, she relented. "Okay, you goofball," she said, rolling her eyes. "I forgive you, but please don't do that again."

"Cross my heart," he swore. This time, when he tried to kiss her, she let him.

***

It was four o'clock by the time she made it back home. Plenty of time to make one of the fancier meals she had planned for her guests. After all, this would be the last time they ate dinner at the inn. Her outing with Cole had been productive. A few stores had managed to restock, and since they needed fewer supplies, they could get what they needed in less time.

After they made up from their fight, they spent the rest of their time together joking around and otherwise having a good time. They even found new costumes for the singles mixer they hosted the next night. It was guaranteed they would be the only ones in costume, but it seemed foolish to waste an opportunity to dress up.

On her way to the kitchen, she discovered Emilio sitting at the dining room table. "Hey," she greeted him. "Did the pottery class end early?"

"What?" he asked, somewhat distracted. "Oh, I don't think so. My interview with Grant ran long, so I missed the class."

"I'm sorry. Do you want me to arrange for you to go tomorrow with Beverly?"

"It's fine," he said, shaking his head.

"Is everything okay?" she asked, concerned.

"Grant offered me the job."

"Congratulations?" she asked hesitantly.

"It's a good thing, I think. Just a lot to take in. I suddenly feel overwhelmed by everything I need to do to make this work.

"Such as?"

"Well, for starters, I need to return to Texas and quit my old job. Then, I need to pack up my apartment, find a new place to live, transfer my bank accounts, the list goes on..."

Grace nodded. "I've never had to do that, but it does sound stressful. Is there anything I can do to help?"

"Do you know of a place to live around here?"

"Are you looking to rent or buy?"

"Rent, at least for now. Can you keep a secret?"

She shrugged. "As long as it won't hurt anyone, sure."

"I like Vanessa. Like, like like her. I thought she came here from another state, too, but I found out she lives about an hour away. Which means, if I move here, we have a chance at a relationship." He sighed. "Although, an hour still seems pretty far."

"How about this? The bed and breakfast will be closed until Easter, so you can rent a room from me for the next couple of months. That will give you time to move here and settle before you make any big decisions about where you'll live."

He thought about it for a minute. "That sounds like a great idea. Are you sure you don't mind?"

"I don't mind. The rent will help me through the lull, and you'll have a place to stay, meals included. Sounds like a win-win to me." She thought about his situation with Vanessa. "How far would you be willing to commute to work each day?"

My current commute can take up to an hour, so I prefer to stay under that. Why?"

"There's a town about thirty minutes west of here. It's a lot bigger than this one, and therefore a lot more expensive, but it's halfway between here and where Vanessa lives..."

"Ooh, I get what you're saying. I'll talk to Vanessa about it. She might be interested in going on a little date to show me around," he grinned. "Thanks, Grace, you're the best."

He got up and left the table, presumably to go to his room to wait for Vanessa.

Her work done, she too got up and continued into the kitchen. She now had less time for dinner but was sure she could still make it work. Tomorrow would certainly be interesting. Her list of singles had now dropped to one. There was always a chance that she, too, could find love. If what they say is true, there's someone out there for everyone.

-Happy Valentine's Day!-

G race arrived at the community center and looked around in wonder. Since she had been too busy for the decorating committee, it was her first time seeing the décor in all its splendor. And it was indeed splendid. Last she had heard, there had been a rift in the committee, with one half wanting to go for a New York City Night Club vibe and the other wanting a more traditional, middle school Valentine's Day dance theme. Luckily, the Night Club had won.

She spotted Cole near the makeshift bar and headed to him, her serving station next door. "Hey," she said when she reached him.

"Hey, yourself," he grinned. He made a show of looking her up and down while whistling. "You look pretty fancy in that outfit, Miss Grace! Sure hope those heels don't end up hurting your feet."

"Whatever pain I endure will be well worth seeing you look at me like that," she said flirtatiously.

He grabbed her hand and spun her around and up against his chest. "Do you really mean that?"

"No," she laughed. "I fully intend to ditch these shoes as soon as I return to my car for the next platter of tarts. But I did wear them for you," she kissed him on the cheek and then walked away. "By the way," she called over her shoulder. "You're looking pretty good yourself."

She smiled to herself as she walked back to her car. Tonight would be a good night; she could feel it. Strong hands wrapped around her waist from behind when she reached the car. Startled, she looked back to see Cole had come up behind her.

"You didn't think I would let you get away with that, did you?" he asked huskily.

"Get away with what?" she asked innocently.

He turned her around and kissed her long and hard. When they finally came up for air, he smiled down at her. "A gentleman would never allow a lady to carry all of these containers herself," he said, grabbing a stack of Tupperware containers from her trunk.

Narrowing her eyes at him, she smacked him on the arm. "A gentleman would never tease a lady like that either."

"Hmm, maybe I'm not as much of a gentleman as I thought."

She rolled her eyes. "Well, because of a certain gentleman, I now need to fix my makeup. Give me a few minutes, and I'll be right behind you."

"Yes, ma'am." He turned around and headed back inside.

After quickly applying a few touch-ups, she changed out of her heels and into less cute but practical flats, grabbed the remaining containers, and went back inside. Grace had volunteered to man the serving table while Cole played the bartender's part. Having continued their theme of choosing old-fashioned serving costumes, they now looked like they stepped out of an early nineteen-hundreds speakeasy.

Bea and Addie had been in charge of providing food for the event, but Bea had called last night in a panic and asked Grace if she could make more of her tarts. Valentine's Day was big business for bakeries, and despite their small-town status, Bea's was no different. Not wanting to let anyone down, Grace agreed and spent half of last night and all day baking. Thankfully, Cole hadn't needed help with his chores that morning.

They worked together to set up their stations, Grace's requiring much more prep work than Cole's. They had just finished up when the first guests of the evening began to arrive. While Grace and Cole were the only ones in costumes, they were not the only ones to dress up. Before long, their singles mixer resembled a fancy gala, with men in suits and women in evening gowns.

"Looks like these people are serious about meeting someone," Grace said into Cole's ear so he could hear her over the music.

"I don't envy them," he replied, watching the crowd. "Hey, aren't those two over there guests at your b-n-b?" he asked, pointing into the crowd.

Grace turned to see where he was pointing and saw Vanessa and Emilio on the dance floor, their bodies so close they were practically glued together. "Yeah, looks like we can take them off the singles list."

Cole nodded. "I suppose. Long distance relationships kind of suck, though."

"Vanessa lives in the city, and Emilio just took a job working for Grant. So..."

"Grant's picking up talent from the b-n-b now?"

Grace shook her head. "Emilio came here for the job interview. All this," she waved her hand around the room, "Was just a bonus."

"Makes sense. I hope it works out for them," he shrugged.

Grace gave him a sideways look. "You're not getting salty on me again, are you?"

In response, he wrapped his arm around her and pulled her close. "I'm sorry," he said, nuzzling her hair. "It's been a long week. I'm tired, and honestly, I want to go home and snuggle with you on the couch while we watch TV or something."

"That sounds wonderful, but unfortunately, we're stuck here," she made a face. A few people wandered over, and they broke apart to serve them. Grace finished before Cole did, so she took the opportunity to watch the crowd. As she scanned the familiar and not-so-familiar faces, she spotted Hunter and Rebekah over in the corner. They did not look happy. In fact, it looked like they were fighting. She knew it was selfish of her, but she hoped they weren't fighting about staying longer. She was more than ready to say goodbye to them tomorrow morning with the rest of her guests.

A few minutes later, they broke apart, and Rebekah stomped over in their direction. She wanted to run, but good manners dictated she stay, so she did her best to smile as she waited for the inevitable.

"This is all your fault," Rebekah screeched when she reached the serving table.

Grace held up her hands and stepped back. "I'm not sure what you're talking about, but maybe we should step outside—"

"I'm not going anywhere with you," she screamed, interrupting Grace mid-sentence. "Before he came back here, Hunter and I were happily planning our future together, but now? Now he's saying he's 'confused,'" she made air quotes with her fingers.

"What does that have to do with me?" A crowd began to form as more and more people became interested in the fight in the corner. She could feel the redness in her cheeks and would have given practically anything for the ability to turn invisible and fade out of existence.

"It has everything to do with you," she yelled. Hunter, who had tried to follow her, finally breached the crowd and rushed to her side. Grabbing her arm, he began to walk toward the exit, pulling her along with him. "She ruined my life, she ruined Hunter's life, and she'll ruin yours too," Rebekah screamed as she pointed at Cole. "If you're smart, you'll dump her before it's too late.

Grace watched Hunter drag her out of the building. At some point, Rebekah had started crying, mascara streaks running down her cheeks. It looked like a scene out of a teen movie where the mean girl finally got her comeuppance. Unfortunately, it wasn't a movie, and instead of everyone clapping and cheering for Grace, they gave her the stink-eye.

Thankfully, the DJ they hired for the event called everyone's attention to the center of the room, where he was starting a dance contest. Luckily for her, the spectators found that more interesting, so they turned away and went back to the party. When Molly appeared a few seconds later, Grace immediately grasped the opportunity to get out of there and bolted out of the event center after thanking Molly profusely.

It wasn't until she reached her car she discovered that she, too, was crying. Her humiliation and anger at the unfairness caused tears of frustration to stream down her cheeks. To add insult to injury, in her haste to leave, she forgot to grab her coat and purse and was now freezing on top of being, once again, locked out of her car.

Since there was no way in this world she was going back in there, she sat down on top of the trunk and buried her face in her hands. Moments later, something warm wrapped around her shoulders, and two strong hands pulled her into his arms, cradling her like a baby. Knowing it was Cole, she wrapped her arms around his neck and held on as he carried her away.

When they reached his truck, he gently put her on the ground, keeping one arm around her waist to steady her. After he quickly unlocked the door, he helped her into the cab, closed the door, and then walked around to the other side to get in. By the time she had composed herself enough to speak, they had maneuvered their way out of the packed parking lot and onto the street.

"Where are we going?" she asked.

"Home," he replied.

"What about my car?"

"We'll get it later."

Nodding, she closed her eyes and rested her head against the window. She was exhausted. The kind of exhaustion one feels in their bones. The weight of everything she had dealt with the last few weeks finally came crashing down, and she felt like she would suffocate beneath its heaviness.

When the truck stopped moving, she opened her eyes to see they were at Cole's farm. She looked at him for the first time since the incident at the community center. "I'm sorry," she said, her voice cracked as tears formed in her eyes and threatened to spill down her cheeks again.

He shook his head, reached across the seat, and pulled her into his arms. "You have nothing to be sorry for," he whispered into her hair, stroking her back.

"You saw how those people looked at me like I'm some kind of home wrecker or something. She said I would ruin your life," Grace choked out between sobs.

"Those people are nothing more than strangers reacting to a drama queen's need to create drama. They don't matter. And I highly doubt you're going to ruin my life," he stated.

"What if you're wrong?"

"I'm not. Grace, look at me," he helped her sit up and cupped the side of her face with his hand. "You are one of the sweetest, kindest, most caring people in the world, who doesn't have a vindictive bone in her entire body. Don't let that woman drag you down into her misery."

"I don't understand why she's so hateful toward me. I've never actually done anything to her," Grace shook her head and wiped her eyes. She was sure she looked horrible, her makeup now a runny, streaky mess. Not at all the way she wanted Cole to see her, especially on Valentine's Day.

"It's easier for her to blame you than to blame Hunter. Because if she blames Hunter, she has to accept that her dreams for the two of them are over. I don't think she's ready to face that yet."

"I don't understand. What does that have to do with me?"

"I'm not an expert, but from what I've seen and heard, there's a good chance Hunter is lost right now and going through a crisis to try to find himself. While a part of him cares for both of you, you each represent a different path that he could take. With you, there's a slower pace of life and a community he can feel a part of. With her, there's the freedom to live life on his own terms and see the world."

"So he never actually liked me; it was what I represented?"

Cole sighed. "I'm not trying to hurt your feelings, but yes. That's only my opinion, though."

"It makes sense," she replied as the events of the last two months played out in her head. "I think that actually makes me feel better. It's less personal than him ditching me the second his plane took off for New York."

Cole sighed again, this time in relief. "I'm glad to hear you say that. Now," he said as he reached into the seat behind him. "I have something for you."

Grace watched as he pulled a bouquet of roses out of the backseat and handed them to her. For the third time that night, tears streamed down her cheeks.

"Are those happy tears?" he asked, concerned.

"Yes, no one's ever given me flowers before," she said, her lip quivering. "I made you your favorite dessert, but it's in the car, so I can't even give it to you," she broke down crying again as she desperately searched her purse for some tissue.

Upon seeing her distress, he opened the door and pulled her out of the truck. "Let's get you inside."

Once inside, she immediately fled to the bathroom and did her best to clean herself up. As she had feared, her makeup had smeared, causing her to resemble the Joker a little too closely for her liking. With nothing left to do, she washed her face and pulled her hair back into a ponytail. Gone was the glamorous look she had spent so much time trying to create.

By the time she returned to the living room, Cole had a fire going in the fireplace. She had completely missed it the last two times she had been there, though, in her defense, it had been dark; now, she looked around the room with fresh eyes. The floors were dark wood with a large, rectangle beige rug in the center. A large TV sat in the corner while a brown sectional lined the wall. A rustic-looking coffee table completed the minimalist look.

"Do you feel better?" he asked, handing her a glass of wine.

Too mesmerized by the flames dancing in his eyes to speak, she nodded.

A slow grin spread across his face. "I think we might owe Rebekah a debt of gratitude," he said mischievously.

"Oh," she raised her brow. "Why's that?"

"Before all that nonsense, I told you all I wanted to do was go home and snuggle with you on the couch. Now, thanks to her, here we are." He sat down and pulled her onto his lap.

She took a sip of wine and placed the glass on the coffee table. "I guess you're right," she said, wrapping her arms around his neck. It was difficult to admit, but at that moment, she didn't care. All that mattered was the two of them were finally alone, safe in their own little world. When their lips finally met, all thoughts of Rebekah, Hunter, and the events from earlier that night vanished from her mind.

"Happy Valentine's Day," she whispered.

"Happy Valentine's Day, baby girl," he whispered back.

The Next Day

It was two o'clock in the morning by the time Grace got home. The decision to go home had been difficult; her desire to stay with Cole and avoid Hunter and Rebekah had warred with her sense of responsibility. In the end, responsibility had won, so here she was, creeping through her house in the middle of the night like a teenager who had stayed out past curfew.

To avoid the creaking front stairs and potentially waking someone up, she went in through the back door and then up the servant's stairs. When she reached the dining room, a large, dark shape at the table made her gasp in surprise. Her gasp of shock caused the shape to move, Hunter's face coming into view as it moved into the moonlight.

"Hunter," she exclaimed, her hand going to her heart. "You almost gave me a heart attack."

"Would serve you right, sneaking around like that," he said irritably.

"Excuse me?" she replied. "What right do you have to judge me? Especially after the stunt your girlfriend pulled tonight?"

"I'm sorry about that," he sighed. He ran his hand through his hair, slumping down in his chair as he did so.

"Apologies aren't going to cut it anymore. I may be running a business, but that does not give her the right to treat me like dirt. Whatever your plans are, she's leaving in the morning."

"Is there any chance for us?" he asked, sorrowful.

"I'm not sure I understand. Chance for what?"

"For us to get back together."

She shook her head. "I'm sorry, but no."

"Because of him?"

"No, because of you. Even if there were no Cole, I could never trust you again. After everything you did to me and everything you allowed Rebekah to do, I don't think I could ever move past that. Those were not the actions of someone who cares about me."

"I never meant for any of this to happen. When I left here, I honestly did plan to go home, pack my things, and return to start my new life. Looking back on my choices, I have no idea how I got to this point."

Grace nodded as her earlier discussion with Cole popped into her head. "I think you need time to figure out what you want. You need space to try new things without pressure to meet someone else's needs."

"You're saying I should break up with Rebekah?"

She shrugged. "Only you can make that decision, but from my point of view, you don't seem very happy with her. Some may consider that my personal bias talking, but it isn't. I still care about you, Hunter, and I want you to be happy. If you decide that you're happy with her, fine. But if not..." she trailed off, her point made.

He was silent for a little bit, her words clearly affecting him. Finally, he nodded to himself as if coming to some conclusion. "We're leaving in the morning. Both of us. I promised her I would give her lifestyle a chance. While what you say makes sense, I will honor that promise."

"I hope it works out for you; I really do."

"Thanks, Grace. For what it's worth, I never meant to hurt you. If I could take it back..."

"Goodbye, Hunter," she said quietly.

"Goodbye, Grace."

She moved into the kitchen and then up the stairs to her room, tears falling freely down her face. Their relationship had only lasted a few weeks, yet she had been more than ready to spend the rest of her life with him. It was apparent now how foolish she had been, but the pain of losing that dream still felt real. The thought she was repeating the same mistake with Cole gave her pause.

Lying on the bed, she thought about all she had shared with Cole over the last few weeks. Yes, there were similarities, but plenty of differences, too. With Cole, she felt like an equal, whereas with Hunter, there was always this feeling he was out of her league. She had initially felt that way with Cole, but he had quickly realized it and disavowed her of that notion. Hunter seemed to thrive on the feeling of being worshiped.

Hopefully, there were other differences; she was too naive and inexperienced to identify them. Only time would tell, but that was something she and Cole had a lot of. Since they lived in the same town, in separate homes, they could explore their relationship without the constraints of distance and the awkwardness of sharing a living space. Whatever happened in the end, for once in her life, she would sit back and enjoy the ride.

***

Eleven o'clock was check-out time, and Grace made sure she was downstairs, ready to say goodbye as her guests left. In a not-so-surprising turn of events, Hunter was gone before breakfast, their conversation the night before his final goodbye. Her feelings were a mixture of relief and sadness. She really did hope he would find happiness someday.

Cole had stopped by, just in case there were any problems with getting 'certain guests' to vacate the premises. Luckily, since Hunter was gone, Rebekah no longer had a reason to stay and seemed more than ready to move on. She never apologized for the night before or any other atrocious behavior on her part. Not that it mattered; Grace wouldn't have believed her anyway.

The guests departed as Grace, Cole, and Molly stood on the porch.

"I guess I'll see you in a couple of weeks," Grace told Emilio.

"Looking forward to it," he replied, his eyes on Vanessa.

"Maybe we'll see you again, too?" Grace asked Vanessa, her brow raised.

"Maybe," she replied, a big smile on her face. "We plan to spend most of our time checking out Hope Springs, but you never know."

"Well, you're always welcome here. Have a safe trip," she waved goodbye as they left.

"I heard you had your share of admirers last night," Grace said to Jane as she stepped onto the porch.

"Just because I don't believe in the commercialization of holidays doesn't mean I don't believe in love," she shrugged.

"Any of the men local?"

"Pretty much all of them. Let's just say my calendar is full for the next month," she winked.

They all laughed.

"It was a pleasure having you as one of my guests," Grace told her. "I hope we get the chance to see you again someday."

"I hope so, too. I'll be in touch. This was a lot of fun." Jane hugged Grace and then walked down the path to her car, waving as she drove off.

Three guests down, one to go. It seemed fitting Rebekah was the first to arrive and the last to leave. When she finally came down the stairs, she was lugging four suitcases, two more than Grace remembered her arriving with. When she saw them standing there, her face turned to one of irritation. "I could use a little help," she snapped.

Ever the gentleman, Cole rushed forward and grabbed her bags, winking at Grace as he walked past her. When

Rebekah moved to follow, Grace stopped her on the stairs. "If you ever get the urge to come here again, don't. You aren't welcome here," Grace told her. "And we'll be watching your social media accounts. We will sue you for defamation if you say anything even remotely negative about us."

"Are you threatening me?" she asked haughtily.

"No, just informing you of the consequences of your actions should you choose to take them."

"Whatever," she rolled her eyes. "As if I would ever come back to this dump anyway."

Grace watched her go, the tension her body had held onto for weeks dissipating with each step Rebekah took. When she was finally gone, they all sighed in relief.

"If I never see her again, it will be too soon," said Molly.

It took a lot of effort, but Grace managed to refrain from saying, 'I told you so.'

"What's next?" asked Cole. "For the b-n-b, I mean."

"Well," Grace replied. "Emilio will be back in a couple of weeks, although from the look of things, he won't be staying here long. Carl's coming for a couple of days next week, and then I suppose it will be time to start planning for Easter."

"Who's Carl?" he asked.

"He's one of the guests that stayed with us at Christmas. You're going to love him," she said, smiling up at him.

"If you two don't mind, now that my office is safe again, I'm going to head down there," Molly interrupted.

They said their goodbyes, Cole taking Grace by the hand and leading her to the porch swing. "I noticed

Hunter wasn't among the departing guests. Does that mean he's still here?"

"No," she shook her head. "He was gone before breakfast. He's decided to travel the world with Rebekah."

"How does that make you feel?"

She thought about it for a minute. "Sad. It was clear he was doing it for her and not because he wanted to."

"If he had chosen you instead?" Cole's expression was neutral, but she could see the side of his mouth twitching in agitation.

"He asked me that last night, so I'll tell you the same thing I told him. There is no chance Hunter and I will ever again have a relationship. My trust in him has been irreparably broken. Not only that," she turned to look at him, grabbed his hands, and held them in hers. "I have never in my entire life felt for someone else what I feel for you. Regardless of what happens between us, I can't go back to a relationship where the feelings are less than."

Cole reached over to cup her face with his hand. "I've never felt this way before either." He kissed the top of her head and pulled her close. "Does this mean we owe Hunter a debt of gratitude too?"

"In a way, maybe. I can't help but feel that even if things had gone according to plan with him, I still would have wanted to be with you. The fact he broke up with me first...well, it certainly made things easier."

Cole's arms tightened around her as he rocked them back and forth with his foot. "It will be nice to have some time together, just the two of us," he finally said, breaking the silence.

"Yeah, I wouldn't mind more nights in front of the fire," she hugged him tightly, memories from the night before flooding her mind.

"I feel like you're reading my mind," he laughed. "Until then, you think Granny and Gladys are up for another game of cards? I'm pretty certain they owe us a re-match."

Grace sat up, looked him straight in the eye, and then pulled his face down to hers, kissing him passionately. When they broke apart, he looked into her eyes. "Not that I'm complaining, but what was that for?"

"For being so wonderful," she said. She stood up, grabbed his hand, and pulled him up with her. "You go get Granny and Gladys, and I'll get the chips and dip. Deal?"

"Deal," he replied. They shook hands as that familiar spark ignited between them. It was crazy to think they had lived in the same town their entire lives but only met a few weeks ago. There's a saying, 'I wish I'd met you sooner so that I could have loved you longer,' and while she certainly understood the sentiment and even agreed with it, she knew in her heart she hadn't been ready to meet Cole until now. She needed to go through the growing pains the last few months had put her through to get to where she was. After all, you can't love someone else until you can love yourself.

For that lesson alone, she would always be grateful to the guests who passed through her life. Each one, in their own unique way, contributed to her personal growth, even Rebekah. The future is never guaranteed, but she finally felt ready to meet it head-on. She looked forward to strengthening the relationships with her loved ones and meeting her newest batch of guests. A new adventure awaits!

Epilogue

One Month Later

Spring had officially arrived, at least for the time being. It was not uncommon in the Midwest to have freezing temperatures and ice storms well into April, but for now, the skies were clear, temperatures were in the seventies, and there were even some flowers beginning to bloom.

Grace was outside enjoying the gorgeous weather when the SUV pulled up to the side of her house, U-Haul in tow. Too excited to wait, she ran to greet him, throwing her arms around his neck as he exited the car. "I'm so excited to see you again!" she exclaimed.

"It's good to see you too," Carl replied, laughing as he returned her hug.

"Do you need help with your bags?" she asked.

"Thanks, but I'm good. I only have one travel bag. Everything else is packed up tight. It's hard to believe that fifty years of my life has been condensed down to one six-by-twelve cargo trailer." He looked at the trailer as he spoke, a mixture of sadness and something else she couldn't quite put her finger on clear in his gaze.

"Hopefully, you only brought the good stuff. While it's good to acknowledge the bad, there's no reason to carry it around with you in the form of literal baggage."

Carl laughed out loud. "Ah, Grace," he said. "I sure have missed your wit and wisdom." He linked arms with her as they walked back toward the house.

"Your room is ready, but I have lemonade and scones on the porch if you want to relax before going inside."

"I'd love that. I've been cooped up in the car for so long; fresh air and basking in the sunlight sound downright heavenly!"

Grace led him to the side porch where the wicker furniture and refreshments awaited. As they sat down, Cole rushed through the front door.

"I'm sorry, babe, but I have to run. One of the mares is foaling, and I need to get over there in case something goes wrong," he kissed her on the cheek and then took off toward his truck.

"Will you be back in time for dinner?" she called after him.

"I'm not sure. I'll text you as the birth progresses," he shouted as he jumped in the truck.

"Sorry about that," Grace smiled at Carl.

"Hunter sure looks different these days," Carl commented noncommittally.

Grace sucked in a deep breath, then let it out slowly. "I guess I never got around to telling you about that." Upon seeing his interest, she told him the story, sparing no detail.

Well, maybe a few details. She didn't think giving him a play-by-play of all the time she'd spent making out with Cole was necessary.

"Wow," he said when she finished her story. "I'm at a loss for what to say. I would have never expected that behavior from the man I met over Christmas."

"That's pretty much been the consensus around here."

"Have you heard from him since he left?"

Grace shook her head. "Grant keeps in touch with him since they're still working together to some extent, but I've asked him not to give me updates. I truly wish Hunter the best, but I felt a clean break was necessary for my own sake."

"I can certainly understand that. From the looks of things, you aren't doing too bad in the romance department these days."

"Nothing to complain about, that's for sure. Hopefully, you'll get to meet Cole later this evening. I'm sure you'll love him as much as I do," she grinned.

"Already in love, eh?"

She shrugged. "Maybe. I meant that more as just a saying, but...," she trailed off as she thought about her feelings. They had never said those words to each other, but in her heart, she knew that if Cole were to say them, she would have no problem saying them back.

Carl reached over to pat her hand. "I'm glad to see you happy, Grace. Take some advice from an old man and try not to overthink it. Love is a beautiful thing."

Smiling, she covered his hand with her free one. "Enough about me; tell me all about New Orleans."

"Ah, New Orleans, the Paris of the West," he said wistfully. "I'm not sure I can put into words the way I felt when I first stepped off the plane. After fifty years, so much had changed, yet so much remained the same. You know about the hurricane and the devastation it wrought, but the spirit of the people remains intact."

"You make it sound so romantic," Grace replied dreamily.

"In a way, it was. I felt a lot like the prodigal son, and I dare say my brother treated me much like the father from that parable. There were a lot of tears, a lot of hugs, and a lot of declarations of regret. After a month of cajoling, I finally agreed to move back permanently."

"What made you come to that conclusion?"

Carl let out a low whistle. "Oh, a lot of things, I suppose. My brother is in poor health, and I'd like to spend the time he has left making up for all the years we lost. Then there's Katherine," he said with a wave. "None of us are exactly spring chickens anymore if you know what I mean."

"Yeah, I know what you mean." Grace thought about Granny and Gladys. They likely wouldn't be sitting on the porch together if it had not been for Granny and Grace's desire to prolong her life. "I sure hope this doesn't mean this will be the last time we'll see you."

"Of course not. I'll make the trip back here at least once a year, and you're always welcome to visit me down there. I would love to show you around sometime. Everyone needs to experience the French Quarter at least once!"

"That sounds wonderful," Grace laughed. "I've always wanted to go to a Mardi Gras parade."

"It's settled then. You'll come out next February, and I'll take you to a parade. Heck, I'll even throw in a king cake for incentive," he replied, his cheerfulness returning.

"Is that the cake with the baby in it?" she asked. "Because I've always wanted to try one of those. They always look so sparkly and pretty."

"That's the one!"

Grace smiled at him, his enthusiasm infectious. She wasn't sure if she could go, what with all her responsibilities, but imagining such a trip would be fun. Some day, she hoped to take him up on his generous offer. For now, she would have to settle for spending what little time they had together. "I feel like I'm hogging all your time," she said. "I know Granny and Gladys are dying to see you again."

"I'm looking forward to seeing the old gals myself. I believe they owe me a card game," he winked.

Grace stood up and collected the tray of refreshments to carry back inside. "Don't let them hustle you this time. They put on a good show of innocence, but those two are card-sharks if I've ever seen them." Grace laughed as she led the way inside.

"Don't worry about me; I've been practicing. Pretty sure I'm gonna give them a run for their money this time."

"Just to warn you, they've been practicing too. I had to talk Cole out of betting his farm. Literally and figuratively."

"I'm so glad I decided to stop by," he laughed. "I've missed this."

"I'm glad you're here too. You're always welcome here. Don't forget that, okay?"

Carl nodded, then headed upstairs to drop his bag off in his room. She wasn't certain, but she was pretty sure he had tears in his eyes. The loss of his partner was still relatively new, and she was convinced that while his reunion with his siblings was a joyous one, there was also a lot of pain. What Carl needed was a break from the sadness. So Grace vowed, then and there, to make his visit the most positive experience of his entire life. Well, she at least wanted it to be up there.

They spent the next few days laughing, telling stories, and playing games. Grace was able to show off her new-found cooking skills, and even Cole was able to get away and spend some time getting to know Carl. From what she could tell, Carl did end up loving Cole. Although, from her point of view, there was little not to love.

Grace felt like she had a real family for the first time in her life. Granny was, of course, her granny, Carl, the father figure she'd always needed. Gladys was the fun aunt, Molly and Grant, the siblings she'd always wished for. Cole, the one she wanted to share it all with. This shows that family isn't defined by blood ties but by the love you have in your heart. And thanks to these people, her heart was overflow-ing.

Afterword

Dear Reader,

Thank you so much for reading *Countdown to Valentine's Day*! When I first wrote *Countdown to Christmas*, Hunter and Grace were my 'it' couple and I had every intention of continuing the series with them as my main characters. Apparently, they had other ideas as when I sat down to write chapter one, they were already on the verge of a breakup. I'm not sure if this happened because as a woman on her second marriage, I sub-consciously made Grace's second chance of love the best one, or if maybe I wanted to do something different. Relationships between a small-town person and a big city person make for a fun read but are rarely sustainable long-term.

Regardless, thank you for coming on this journey with me, Grace, Cole, Molly, and the rest of the gang. If you want to find out what happens next, *Countdown to Easter* is available on all major retailers as well as on my site at d iannahouxshop.com. If you'd like access to weekly emails, updates, behind-the-scenes content, giveaways, and more, go to diannahoux.com and sign up for my newsletter. You will receive a copy of Lessons from a Jilted Bride which contains characters you will meet again in the coming books.

Happy Reading!

-Dianna

About the Author

Dianna is a wife, mother, reader, writer, and small-town girl at heart. She resides in a rural Missouri town of less than twenty-five hundred people with her husband and three boys in a late 1800s home they've been lovingly restoring when she isn't busy working on her next book.

A romantic at heart, she believes in happily-ever-afters rooted in realism and, most importantly, humor!

She is the author of Forsaking the Dark, a paranormal romance, The Queen's Revenge, a historical romance, and the Holiday Countdown Series, a sweet, small-town romance series.

Made in United States
Cleveland, OH
13 June 2025

17704616R10127